# *Five Faces West*

**Raymond D. Mason**

# *Five Faces West*

Copyright © 2013 by Raymond D. Mason

Raymond D. Mason books may be ordered through authorized booksellers or by contacting:

You may order books through:
www.Amazon.com
www.CreateSpace.com
www.Waldenbooks.com
www.Target.com

E-Books available through:
www.Amazon.com
www.Smashwords.com

or personalized autographed copies from:
E-mail: RMason3092@aol.com

(541) 679-0396

This is a work of fiction. All characters, names, incidents, organizations, and dialogue in this novel are either the products of the author's imagination or are used fictitiously.

Printed in the United States of America

## **Dedication**

This book is dedicated to all those who have purchased my books, be it e-book readers or those who have purchased the paperbacks. I want to take this opportunity to thank each and every one of you for your support. The highest compliment a person can give a struggling author is to purchase one or more of their books.

I enjoy hearing from those who have purchased my books and try to respond personally to each e-mail. My e-mail address is rmason3092@aol.com so feel free to drop me a line. I'd love to hear from you.

Raymond D. Mason

# **Preface**

Identical twins, Brent and Brian Sackett, fought in the War Between the States on opposite sides. When the War was over Brian returned to the family ranch in Taylor County, Texas; but Brent, bitter from the family divide brought on by the War, took a job as a deputy sheriff in Crystal City, Texas.

Brent's anger ate away at him until it eventually drew him into breaking the law. After shooting a man who had robbed a freight office in Crystal City, Brent hid the stolen money in order to return later and retrieve it. When caught red handed by the sheriff, Brent shot and killed him, thereby making him a man on the run with a price on his head.

At the very same time AJ Sackett, Brent and Brian's older brother, was shot and severely wounded by two men who worked for John Sackett, the head of that branch of the Sackett family. The men who had actually shot AJ placed the blame on another man who had just been fired by AJ. Brian struck out to bring the accused man to justice.

Brian unknowingly traveled a very similar route taken by his identical twin brother and was mistaken for his now, outlaw brother. Their trails eventually crossed and there was a bitter/sweet reunion before Brent was forced to make a daring escape from the law once again.

Brian returned to the family ranch, while Brent continued to drift from one town to the next always just one jump ahead of the law. It was while on the dodge that Brent met Julia; a woman who had almost been killed when cowboys working for a ruthless rancher murdered her husband and those traveling with them to Sundown, Texas.

Brent nursed the woman back to health and in the process fell in love with her. He promised her that he would get her to Sundown where her husband and his brother had purchased a small farm. Just before arriving there, however, Brent was seriously wounded by two bank robbers and teetered on the edge of death.

When word reached the Sackett ranch that Brent might be holed up in Lubbock County, Brian and AJ set out to find their wayward brother and see if they could help him. Events led them to Sundown and they eventually connected with Brent and Julia.

The couple had decided that California might be the safest place for them, but agreed to going back to the Sackett ranch with Brian and AJ and seeing the rest of the family before making the move out West. Brent's plans changed, however, when Julia helped deliver a baby that was being born breach; she saved the baby, but was unable to save the life of the baby's mother.

Not being able to keep up his homestead and take care of a baby too, the young father, Grant Holt, accepted the invitation to make the move to California with Brent and Julia. Julia now had a baby to take care of and would soon learn she was carrying one of her own. Brent felt it would be better for them to go to California without returning to see the Sackett family.

Brian and AJ returned to the ranch and explained to the rest of the family about Brent's decision. They were all pleased that the rift that had separated them had finally been somewhat mended. Our story picks up with Brent and Julia joining up with a wagon train headed west to California.

For the story leading up to this segment in the Sackett series see the fourth book entitled, "Range War".

# Chapter

# 1

**10 Miles West of
Seminole Draw, Texas**

**Brent Sackett** smiled when he saw the wagon train off in the distance. **Julia** was in the back of the covered wagon tending to the Holt baby while **Grant Holt**, the baby's father, rode along side the wagon and talked to Brent.

"There it is, Grant," Brent said nodding towards the long line of wagons. "We'll be able to make camp tonight and feel safe about going to sleep," Brent said with a grin.

"I've heard that some wagon master's don't like picking up folks along the way. They're afraid they may be part of a gang that wants to rob them," Grant said.

"You'll hear all kinds of stories about wagon trains. I've even heard tales of wagon masters leading their train into ambushes so they could make off with the families valuables. Most of the stories are nothing more than someone's imagination though," Brent replied.

"When we came out to Texas there were four wagons; that's all. Grace and I joined up with three families that were making the move to the Dallas area. We made the last leg of our trip on our own," Grant said taking on a look of sadness at the mention of his deceased wife.

Brent could understand Grant's sense of loss due to the deep feelings he now had for Julia. He could just imagine how he would feel if he was to lose her. Death is so permanent; so final.

Hoping to keep Grant from sinking deeper into his thoughts, Brent said, "You know what I've heard, Grant; I've heard that some of these wagon trains have hoe downs on a nightly basis. There're always folks who can play a fiddle, a guitar, or a squeeze box and are ready to play at the drop of a hat."

Grant smiled slightly and looked again in the direction of the wagon train.

"That train is sure big enough to have a few musicians traveling with it," he said. "How many wagons have you counted?"

"I counted thirty three, but then I noticed a few more wagons straggling behind. I'd say thirty six...maybe thirty seven," Brent said.

Just then he heard Julia giggle as she held baby Gracie.

"You are so cute; yes you are. You are just too cute," Julia said.

"Thank you, honey; so are you," Brent said with a grin.

"Not you, you big lug; I was talking to the baby," Julia said knowing full well that Brent was joking.

"Oh...hey, I'm glad that is a little girl you're making over. If it was a boy I might get jealous," Brent laughed.

"You know better than that, Brent. No other man could ever take your place," Julia said with a warm smile.

"You'll have some women folk to talk to tonight," Brent said.

"How far away is the wagon train?"

"A couple of miles; it won't be long until we meet up with them," Brent answered.

"It will be nice to talk to some women with children. I've got a number of questions to ask them about Gracie and the one I'm carrying," Julia said.

"I'm a little worried about what will happen when we hit some rough spots along the trail. I hope you'll be okay," Brent said seriously.

"Don't worry; I'll be fine. If anything, I worry about how this baby will make it."

"Grant is really a fine young fella, ain't he," Brent said as he glanced up ahead where Grant had ridden.

"He is at that. I sure feel sorry for him. He's holding his sorrow over losing Grace inside and I'm sure it's eating him up," Julia said thoughtfully.

"He's tough; he'll make it," Brent said.

"You men...you're always so unflappable when it comes to showing your feelings over something," Julia said giving Brent a slightly accusing look.

"We have feelings; we're just not as emotional about it as you women. Hey, I've had tears in my eyes a number of times," Brent replied.

Julia made a face, "Tears in your eyes! When is the last time you had a real good cry?"

"Ah...Tears in a man's eyes is the same thing," Brent argued.

"Not likely," Julia said and laughed.

"If you don't quit picking on me I think I'll just throw myself on the ground and start kicking and screaming and clawing my eyes out, while I cry, cry, cry," Brent said and then laughed.

Julia laughed too.

Brent and Julia's wagon reached a spot ahead of the wagon train and waited for the train's lead wagon to approach them. Brent waved at the man driving the team and another man on horseback alongside it.

"Howdy, where you folks headed," Brent called out?

"We're goin' to California; to the Sacramento Valley."

"We're headed out that way too. Would you mind if we took up a spot at the rear of the train. We'd sure be mighty obliged," Brent said.

"Yeah, you folks are welcome to join us. Just pull your wagon in at the end of the train," the wagon master said, and then asked, "What're you folk's names?"

Brent paused for a second and then said, "My name is Brent Johnson and this is my wife Julia. The young man there is Grant Holt and this is Little Gracie. The baby belongs to Grant...he lost his wife shortly after she'd given birth," Brent explained.

"I'm sorry to hear that. My name is Major John Harper Dupree and this is Jim Bowers, our scout. We're glad to have you folks join us. I'll get with you once we make camp tonight and go over our rules and introduce you to the others traveling with us at that time."

"Thanks a lot, Major. We really appreciate you taking us on," Brent said as he shook the major's hand and then asked. "Is Major part of your name or rank?"

"It's a carry over from the War. I fought for the Confederacy even though I knew it was a losing cause from the very start. There was just too much against us," the major said.

"I see. I wish I'd met you before I joined up; I might have made a different decision," Brent said with a half grin.

"It was a rough decision on everyone's part, I'd say," the major said just before the baby started to fuss.

The major looked towards Julia who was holding baby Gracie and said, "The women will be thrilled that there is a newborn traveling with us. They'll probably all want a hand in helping your lady with the baby," the major said with a smile.

"Babies do that to women, don't they," Brent laughed.

The major looked serious and paused for a moment, "I want you to know that we're taking a different route from a lot of the other wagon trains. We're going to be going up to Santa Fe and take the Old Spanish Trail north to a trail I know that will connect us with the California Trail. It hasn't seen much use for quite a long spell, but I've ridden it on horseback and for where we want to go, I think it's the best route to take."

"I see," Brent said thoughtfully. "I figured you be taking the Southern Emigrant Trail out of Mesilla to Tucson and then on into Los Angeles," Brent said and then added, "Is your way safer?"

"It's as safe as any of them. I figure no one will be expecting to see a wagon train on that old route, so it could be somewhat safer than the others," the major replied.

"You're the wagon master," Brent said and forced a smile.

Just then a man from one of the other wagons rode his saddle horse up where the major was and asked angrily, "What's the holdup, Major?"

The major responded quickly, "These folks are going to join the train, Dean."

"Fine, but keep moving while we've still got daylight; we're wasting time," Jacob Dean snapped.

Brent gave the man a hard look and took an instant disliking towards him. Dean returned the look. The two men's eyes locked on to one another and a fuse of animosity was lit between them. It would just be a matter of time before the two of them would lock horns and they both knew it.

"Just take your spot at the rear of the train, folks. We'd better get to moving again," the major said.

Brent held the team aside and let the other wagons pass by, getting friendly looks and smiles from most. A few of the men didn't seem too happy with the new addition, however. Once the last wagon had passed Brent pulled their team and wagon in behind it.

It didn't take long for Brent to understand why there had been some stragglers at the tail end of the wagon train. Dust from the wagons ahead of them was enough to force the last wagons to drop back a ways to have a little better breathing room.

Julia made over baby Gracie like she was her own. With every cry or whimper Julia was right there to make sure the baby was all right. Brent could not hold back the smile as he thought of the love Julia had brought into his life, and now into the life of that little one.

Grant Holt was a fine young man. He appeared to be of good, strong character and was always ready to lend a helping hand to someone in need. Grant seemed to know what needed to be done and was quick to do them; something that impressed Brent greatly.

Brent felt much more at ease now that they were on their way to California and traveling with a wagon train. Those looking for him would have a much harder time finding him now. Once they were out of Texas the chances of discovery would be even less; or so he hoped.

There was one thing that bothered Brent; something he kept to himself. He'd heard stories about wagons heading West on the Old Spanish Trail being hijacked by bandits. Indian activity was not quite as bad as it had been years earlier, but there was always the chance of renegade bands from the various tribes.

He didn't want to upset Julia though, so he decided to keep his concerns strictly to himself; not even sharing them with Grant. The major seemed like a decent sort, therefore, Brent didn't think he might be leading the wagons into a trap. Only time would tell.

**Raymond D. Mason**

# Chapter

# 2

## Pine Spring Relay Station, Texas

**Black Jack Haggerty** topped a hill and looked down on the Pine Spring Overland Stage Line relay station. Here he figured he could get something to eat and maybe a drink of whiskey.

Haggerty headed down the gentle slope at a leisurely pace. He'd been pushing the horse he'd stolen from a family of homesteaders hard and the horse needed a rest badly.

Off to Haggerty's left he saw a stagecoach approaching the relay station and his first thought was about the money the coach might be carrying. He quickly dispelled that thought when he noticed the five saddle horses tied up in front of the station house.

The stagecoach arrived before Haggerty did and the passengers were being unloaded when he rode up. Jack cast a quick glance at the saddle horses and noticed a US Cavalry brand on the right flank of one of the horses. The horse may have belonged to the cavalry, but the saddle certainly didn't; it was a Western saddle not a cavalry issue.

Haggerty stepped down off his mount and looked towards the last passenger stepping down out of the coach. It was a woman; a beautiful woman, to be sure. She cast a casual glance in his direction and then flashed a demure smile his way.

Haggerty tied the bridle reins to the hitching rail and dusted himself off before entering the building. The five saddle horses caused Haggerty some concern. He adjusted his gun belt before opening the door and entering.

Jack spotted the riders of the five horses quickly enough. They were hard cases, to be sure. One of the men looked vaguely familiar to Jack. He couldn't put a time and a place where he'd seen the man, but he felt sure that he had seen him before.

The five men were seated at a long table next to the one occupied by the coach passengers. Haggerty walked up to the small bar that was in a corner of the room and ordered a beer.

When Haggerty looked back towards the table where the five men were seated, he found them all looking his way. He nodded slightly and then looked towards the other table where the beautiful woman passenger was sitting. She was watching him with a curious eye.

"That'll be a dime," the man behind the bar said.

"A dime; I can get a beer for a nickel in any saloon in Texas," Haggerty commented.

"Well, wait until you get to one of them saloons then," the man said unperturbed.

Haggerty grinned and replied, "As thirsty as I am, I'd go a dollar for a good beer."

"Nope, just a dime," the man said evenly.

Haggerty took a long drink of the beer and once again glanced at the five hard cases. One of the men was still watching him; it was the man Haggerty thought he'd seen before.

The man had a look about him that indicated trouble. He wore a heavy moustache and his hat was pushed back and held by a draw string around his neck. His trousers were black and he wore a red shirt with a row of buttons down each side. A bandana was tied loosely around his neck.

As Haggerty stood there drinking his beer the man got to his feet and adjusted the two guns he was wearing. With the other men watching him, he walked over to where Haggerty was standing.

"Howdy..., I can't help but think that I've seen you somewhere before," the man said quietly.

Haggerty looked him up and down and answered, "Yeah, I was thinking the same thing about you."

"Where do you hail from," the young man asked?

"No place in particular," Haggerty replied. "I drift around a lot,"

"Yeah, we do too. Have you ever been around Dallas?"

"Yeah, I've been around Dallas, Abilene, Wichita, Dodge City, Amarillo, San Antonio, Houston, Like I said, I drift around a lot," Haggerty answered.

"You wouldn't be 'Black Jack' Haggerty by any chance would you," the stranger asked?

"Who's asking," Haggerty replied with a frown?

The man looked around to make sure no one was listening in on their conversation. The only one who was paying them any attention was the woman seated with the passengers at the other table and out of ear shot.

"The name's Johnny Ringo...maybe you've heard of me?"

Haggerty grinned slightly and nodded his head slowly, "Yeah I've heard of you. The Hoodoo War if memory serves me correctly. It's nice to make your acquaintance, Ringo. Yeah, I'm Black Jack Haggerty."

Ringo looked around before asking, "Would you care to join us? We might have something you'd be interested in."

"Yeah, I don't mind if I do. I'll tell you one thing, though; if what you've got planned is something around these parts I ain't interested. I'm a little on the 'warm' side...if you get my drift," Haggerty grinned.

"Oh, a bank, coach, or train," Ringo asked?

"Cattle...not as many as I'd hoped, but enough when you get the right price," Haggerty stated as the two walked to the long table!

"Have a seat and meet the boys," Ringo said. Then, just loud enough for those at their table to hear added, "Men, I'd like for you to say hello to 'Black Jack' Haggerty."

The others nodded their heads in recognition of Haggerty's name and a couple said "Howdy" or "Hey."

"Jack, this is 'Curly Bill' Brocius...next to him is Pete Spence, better known as Eliot Ferguson, then

Frank Stillwell,...and last but not least is Duke McDowell," Bass said.

"Howdy men," Haggerty said and sat down next to McDowell. "So what is it you wanted to tell me about," Haggerty then asked?

"We're headed for Arizona Territory. We hear that there's a ton of money to be made out there. Frank, here, knows a ranch owner down there who has a going concern. He needs some gun hands and we're providing them. We could always use a man of your caliber," Ringo said with a grin.

"Sounds tempting, Johnny; in fact, I'm on my way to Arizona myself. I've got the law looking for me all over Texas and I need to rest up and let the heat die down. I may even head on out to California if I don't see anything I like in Arizona," Haggerty said.

"From what I hear there's a lot to like in Arizona. That is...if you like money," Ringo said, getting a laugh from the others.

"If it's so great in Arizona what are you boys doing in Texas," Jack asked?

"Getting out of it as soon as possible," Ringo said, and then added. "We had a little business to take care of here; now that we've taken care of it, it's Arizona."

"Let me think it over. If I decide to fall in with you boys, and the offer is still open, I'll let you know," Haggerty stated and then asked, "What's this rancher's name you're going to work for?"

"Old Man Clanton, down near Bisbee; maybe you've heard of him," Ringo replied?

"Nope, can't say as I have," Haggerty said, and casually glanced at the next table.

The woman from the stagecoach was still eyeing him with a curious eye. Jack nodded and tipped his hat, to which she nodded slightly in return.

"Looks like you might have found something you like right here," Ringo said noticing the gesture.

"It does at that," Haggerty replied. "I'm sure you're used to dealing with things like that, also," Haggerty grinned?

"Enough; I think it's the devil in us that they like. Angels aren't nearly as much fun," Ringo chuckled.

"Well, if you'll excuse me I think I'll play the devil's advocate and see what this little lady wants."

"If you decide to join us just ask around Bisbee where the Clanton ranch is and anyone in the area can tell you how to find it," Ringo said.

"I'll do that. Nice meetin' you boys," Haggerty said as he got up, getting nods from the other men.

Haggerty walked over to where the woman was seated. She watched him intently as he moved towards her. Haggerty cocked one eyebrow slightly and when he got to her table sat down next to her.

"So, what is a girl like you doing in a nice place like this," Haggerty said with a charming smile?

"What...I think you have that a little mixed up," the woman said returning his smile. "...but then, maybe you don't. You tell me what you're doing here and I'll think about telling you what I'm doing here."

"Oh, a thinking woman, huh," Haggerty replied. "If we're going the same way we might travel together."

"I'm on my way to Tucson," the woman said.

"Well, bless my soul...I'm on my way to Tucson, also. What do you say we travel together," Haggerty suggested?

"I don't know the least thing about you. Why...what would people think?"

"I don't care what people think. If anyone asks we'll just tell them we're married," Haggerty grinned.

"That would suggest several things, don't you think," the woman replied.

"We could cover a couple of those things before anyone even asked," Haggerty said with a shrug of his shoulders.

"Like what?"

"We could get to know one another on a more intimate level. I'm willing if you are," Haggerty went on.

"What if I am? How would we travel? You weren't on the stagecoach with me; so you must be traveling by horseback. I don't travel by horseback. I prefer a much more comfortable mode of transportation," the woman said.

"That's no problem. I'll just ride along with the stagecoach on into El Paso. We'll get a double horse and carriage and travel on to Tucson in style. What do you think," Haggerty asked with a wry smile?

"It's tempting...let me think about it. I'll have a long ways to make up my mind as to what I should do," she replied coyly.

Haggerty held up his hands, "Hey, that's only fair. I can act as a guard for the valuable cargo the stagecoach is hauling."

The woman looked puzzled, "Oh, valuable cargo? I hadn't heard that."

Haggerty smiled seductively, "That valuable cargo is you, pretty lady."

"You sure know how to turn a woman's head, Mister...," she said.

"Haggard, Jack Haggard; and you are?"

"Miss Bonita Brand," the woman said.

"Brand...do you have one? A brand, that is," Haggard said with a grin.

"When we get to know one another better...I might let you see it," Bonita said lowering her eyelids seductively.

"El Paso...here we come."

# Chapter 3

### Pima County, Arizona
### X-X Ranch Bunk House

**Lincoln Sackett** stared at his poker hand for several seconds and then picked up a dollar and tossed it into the poker pot.

"See your fifty cents and raise you fifty cents, Hoyle," Linc said.

"I wish you wouldn't do that, Linc; I ain't won but one pot all night. I was hoping you'd let me have this one," Hoyle said in a slightly whining voice.

"I might be bluffing, Hoyle," Linc said with a grin.

Hoyle looked at his hand and then over to Buck Benton, the ranch foreman and asked, "What do you think, Buck; should I see him?"

"Hey, leave me out of this, Hoyle. I don't want you blaming me if you lose this hand," Buck said holding his hands up defensively.

"Shorty, what do you think...see, raise, or fold," Hoyle pressed?

Shorty who was seated next to Hoyle said, "I'd see Linc's bet."

Hoyle grinned as he tossed a fifty cent piece into the pot and said, "I'll see that and call."

Linc grinned as he laid a pair of King's. A big grin came to Hoyle's face and he gave Shorty a quick glance and elbow to the little man's arm.

Hoyle lay his cards down and showed a straight with Jack high. He started to reach for the pot when Linc said, "Huh uh...I wasn't finished yet, Hoyle. Here're three Deuces to go with those Kings."

Hoyle dropped his head in defeat as Link dragged in the pot of four dollars and seventy five cents. Linc watched Hoyle for a few seconds and then said with a chuckle, "I'll tell you what I'll do, Hoyle. The next time we go to Muldoon's your drinks will be on me; how's that?"

Hoyle grinned widely, "You're Aces in my book Linc. I guess I don't mind losing to you nearly as much as I do to the rest of these 'tenderfeet'," Hoyle said looking at the other three men at the table with Linc and him.

"That's it for me," one of the men said.

"Me too," another said.

That left just Hoyle, Linc, and a young man by the name of **Jory Tatum**. Jory was a quiet young man who seemed to be deep in thought most of the time. No one had been able to get close to the young man, but not for a lack of trying. He just didn't want to have much to do with the rest of the men. The poker playing on that night was unusual for him.

"Are you still in Jory," Linc asked?

"I'm still sittin' here ain't I," Jory said.

Linc looked at him questioningly for a moment and then looked at Hoyle, "What about you Hoyle?"

"Yeah, I'm a glutton for punishment. Maybe if I lose enough you'll buy me a good dinner when we go to Muldoon's," Hoyle said with a wry grin.

"You can't buy a 'good' dinner at Muldoon's, Hoyle, you know that," Linc laughed and then said, "It's your deal Jory," and set the deck in front of him.

"Same game," Jory stated.

"Where'd you come from, Jory," Linc asked merely making small talk.

"No place in particular," Jory replied tersely.

Linc continued to gaze at this quiet man. After several more silent seconds, Linc stated, "I notice a little bit of a Texas drawl. Ever been to Texas, Jory?"

"Yeah, I've been there. Weren't much there," Jory said closed mouth.

"Ain't much there? Man, that is one big state to say there weren't much there," Hoyle said as though shocked by the statement.

"Weren't much where I was," Jory said.

"Where were you...in jail," Hoyle pressed jokingly?

Jory looked up at Hoyle and snapped angrily, "Yeah, what if I was in jail; what are you going to do about it, huh?"

"Hey, hold on, hoss," Linc said quickly, "I'm sure Hoyle didn't mean anything by it."

Hoyle looked shocked, "No, Jory...I didn't mean anything by it. I hope I didn't insult you...sure didn't mean to if I did."

25

Linc gave Jory a hard stare. Usually someone who refuses to talk about where they came from has something to hide. He'd wondered about Jory from the first day they'd met, but didn't want to judge him too quickly.

Jory got up from the table and picked up his money. He shoved the bills and change into his pocked and looked around the table.

"I'm through; I've had it," he said, turned and walked away.

Buck stood up and said firmly, "I think it's time we all turned in. We've got a busy day tomorrow, getting ready for the upcoming cattle drive. See you boys in the morning," he said.

Hoyle watched Jory as he walked to his bunk at the back of the bunkhouse.

"I didn't mean to upset him, Linc; honest I didn't," Hoyle said apologetically.

"I know you didn't Hoyle; don't worry about it. Jory has been hiding something from day one. You weren't out of line," Linc said sincerely.

"Thanks, Linc. Sometimes I think you and Buck are the only sane ones around here. With the exception of me that is," Hoyle said.

"Oh yeah...that's understood," Linc said with a grin and then added. "Well, let's turn in and get ourselves a good night's sleep; what do you say?"

"Sounds good to my weary old bones," Hoyle answered.

"G'night," Linc said and walked to his bunk.

Linc lay down on his bed and stared up at the ceiling. He had tried to get to know young Tatum, but it was obvious Tatum wanted no one getting close to him. It was too bad; everybody needs someone they can confide in. It seemed Tatum had no one.

As the tall cowboy lay there his eye lids grew heavy and he was soon sound asleep. Linc dreamed of green fields of high grass and fat, contented cattle grazing peaceably along the banks of a river brimming with catfish. Life was good and peaceful...in his dream.

**Raymond D. Mason**

# Chapter 4

**Ten miles from the
Texas/New Mexico Border**

The wagon train covered about ten to twelve miles a day. Brent, Julia, and Grant had met a number of families and felt accepted by them. About five days out, however, Brent recognized a man he'd first met while working as a deputy sheriff in Crystal City.

Brent had been in a couple of poker games with the man, but for the life of him couldn't remember the man's name. It was obvious the man hadn't recognized Brent, though, not yet anyway; probably due to the fact Brent was sporting a moustache now.

Julia had noticed how Brent watched the man that night when everyone was gathered around in the middle of the circled wagons. She didn't ask him about it right away, but her curiosity continued to build as the evening wore on. Finally she had to know why Brent was so intent on the man.

"Brent, do you know the man with the large moustache and the Derby hat, sitting over there by himself," she asked?

Brent looked at her for a moment before answering, "Yes, I've seen him before when I was a deputy sheriff, but I don't think he has recognized me; not yet, anyway. He may not know I'm on the run, because if my memory serves me correctly, he left Crystal City before I had my trouble there."

"What will we do if he should recognize you," Julia questioned.

"I don't know; we'll have to cross that bridge when we come to it."

"Let's pray he doesn't remember you."

"Yeah, let's do that," Brent said and then smiled just as one of the fiddlers in the group started playing a rousing little jig and was soon joined by other musicians.

"Dance with me, Brent," Julia said grabbing Brent's hands and pulling him to his feet.

With a laugh Brent began to twirl Julia around the large circle to the hoots and hollers of the crowd. Soon other couples joined them and a good old fashioned hoe down was underway.

As Brent and Julia whirled around the circle, Brent caught an occasional glimpse of the man whose name escaped him. The man seemed to be watching them more than the others who were dancing. This bothered Brent.

Just as the tune that had started the folks dancing ended, Brent remembered the man's name he'd seen in Crystal City. It was Dobbs; **Denver Dobbs**. He was a card sharp out of Denver, Colorado; thus the nickname 'Denver'.

Brent and Julia sat down, both wearing wide grins on their faces. Life had become fun for Brent since he'd met and fallen in love with Julia. He knew in his heart that she was a godsend.

The music started another upbeat tune as some folks sat down and others got up to dance. Brent got up to fetch a pillow for Julia out of the back of the wagon.

"You two can really cut a rug," a man's voice said while Brent's back was turned.

Brent turned around quickly and found himself looking into the face of Denver Dobbs.

"Would you mind if I danced with your lady fair," Dobbs asked politely while tipping his hat?

The smile quickly dropped from Brent's face as he looked at the man and then quickly at Julia.

"I don't know if she's up to it," Brent replied seriously. "She's in the family way."

"Oh, I can dance one more dance I think," Julia said and gave Brent a slight wink.

"It's up to her then; but be careful with her," Brent said taking on a more serious tone of voice.

"I'll certainly do that...Ma'am," Dobbs said as he held out his hand to help Julia to her feet.

Julia and Dobbs began to dance around to the beat of the music with Brent watching every move. Dobbs held Julia at arms length, which met with Brent's approval. The look on Brent's face was one of concern mixed with a twinge of jealousy at seeing another man dancing with his woman.

Dobbs acted as the perfect gentleman and once the music stopped escorted Julia back over to where Brent was waiting.

"Thank you, Ma'am," Dobbs said, "and thank you for allowing me the pleasure of dancing with your lady."

Brent nodded his head slowly as Dobbs gave him a serious eyeing and then asked, "Have we met somewhere before? My name is Dobbs, Denver Dobbs."

"I don't think so; the name doesn't ring a bell," Brent replied.

"I get the feeling I've seen you, but for the life of me I can't remember where or when," Dobbs said.

"Oh...I can't help you. I don't remember ever having seen you," Brent said evenly.

"Well, no matter. Thanks again, Ma'am. I enjoyed that whirl."

Dobbs walked back to where he'd been sitting with Brent staring holes in his back. Julia watched Brent and finally broke the silence.

"He won't remember you. If he's a gambler he's seen too many men's faces to remember where he's seen them all, unless something unusual happened, that is. Did anything unusual happen while the two of you were playing cards," Julia asked?

"No, nothing I can recall."

"He told me that he's going to California to start up a saloon in San Jose. He'll be leaving the wagon train before long. He said he's been to California before and the Southern Emigrant Trail is a lot easier," Julia said relaying on to Brent what she'd learned from Dobbs.

"He told you that while you were dancing," Brent asked with a curious look?

"Yep, he did."

Brent thought about Dobbs' statement to Julia for a moment and then said, "I'd heard the Southern Trail is the best, most direct route. Maybe, just maybe we'll be leaving the wagon train before too long, too."

Just then little Gracie began to fuss a little and Julia quickly started to attend to her. While she did that, Brent watched and thought about this Denver Dobbs. Something didn't set right with Brent about Dobbs, but he couldn't put his finger on it. He'd have to keep an eye on the man; that was for sure.

**Raymond D. Mason**

# Chapter 5

### The Sackett Ranch

**Brian** and **AJ Sackett** were busily trying to get a calf out of the muck and mire the Indians called 'Black Water'. To them it was just a 'bog'. In reality it was a pool of crude oil, but unbeknownst to them at the time.

"Man, I wish calves had brains enough to stay out of this stuff," Brian said as he pushed on the calf's rump while AJ pulled on the rope they'd put around its neck.

"You and me both, little brother," AJ fumed.

Once freed the calf wobbled off to find its mother and the two brothers looked at one another and began to laugh.

"You look a fright," Brian said.

"You don't look any better. Let's go down to Clear Fork Creek and clean up," AJ suggested.

"What's holding you back," Brian said as he headed in the direction of the creek.

It was only about a half mile to the creek and although there had been a long dry spell there was still enough water to take a bath in. When the two brothers arrived they wasted no time in diving into the water; clothes and all.

Once they were able to rinse some of the oil out of their clothes they climbed out and hung them on a fallen tree limb to dry. They went back into the water and took a good bath, sans clothes.

While they were cavorting in the cool water, two wagons from a traveling medicine show happened along. There were two men and three women traveling together. One of the men was Professor Hubert Tyler Blythe, III and the other man was a trick shot artist with the show who went by the name 'Buffalo Benny' Hart.

The three women did specialty dances and worked the crowds for whatever contributions they could get...or pockets they could pick. When they saw the two men bathing, the women began to give out with catcalls.

Brian and AJ stood in the water that was just over waist high and looked at the curious onlookers. Finally AJ called out to them, "Ain't you ever seen grown men taking a bath before?"

"Not as handsome as you two," one of the women yelled back. "Come on out and give us a good look?"

"Never you mind," AJ said and then added, "Why don't you three join us? The water's fine."

"It looks it; maybe we will," the woman said getting laughter from the other two women.

"What are you selling, anyway," AJ called to the man in the lead wagon?

"Whatever it is that you might be in need of, gentlemen," the professor said with a flourish. "I'd say you might be in need of some clean, dry clothes about now; am I right?"

"Yeah, that should go without saying," AJ said looking at Brian with a grin.

"I've got just what you need and I'll give you a good deal on them," the professor said with a head shake.

"Well, we can't come out to take a look at them. How about holding 'em up so we can see them from here," Brian said.

"Sure thing," the professor said and disappeared behind the canvas flap.

Brian and AJ were busy watching for the professor when they heard several loud splashes in the water behind them. They turned around and saw the three women just coming up out of the water.

"You're right, this water is fine," one of the women said.

Brian and AJ looked at one another as their faces broke into big grins. The women had their undergarments on and were splashing around like three kids at their favorite swimming hole on a hot August day.

"Hey, that's no fair, ladies," AJ called out.

"What ain't fair, honey," one of the women asked?

"You got your clothes on and we ain't," AJ replied.

"Well, we can fix that, honey child," one of the women said and the three of them doffed their undergarments.

The professor emerged from the back of the wagon and held up two pairs of pants and two work shirts. When he saw the women cavorting with Brian and AJ in the water he called out in an agitated voice.

"Ladies, we don't have time for this. We've got a long way to go. Now come along and get out of there; business before pleasure," he said firmly.

"Come on gals, I'm gettin' hungry and you're holding things up," the trick shot artist said.

The three women complained as they gathered their garments and waded back in the direction of their wagon they had stopped in the middle of the stream. AJ and Brian watched as they climbed out of the water and into the wagon before getting dressed.

The two brothers looked at one another and smiled from ear to ear as they shook their heads.

"They ain't going to believe us back at the ranch," AJ said.

"Hey, you and the boys didn't believe the story I told you about what happened to me outside of San Antonio; so why should they believe this," Brian agreed.

Then AJ called to the professor, "Hey, we'll take those clothes if they fit. Hold on while we get you some money."

"Oh, we'll get the money; you just stay right where you are. I see where your clothes are hanging on the downed tree limbs. Don't worry, gentlemen; you can trust Professor Hubert Tyler Blythe, III as far as the East is from the West."

Before the brothers could argue Buffalo Benny was down on the ground and running to the downed tree where he went through their pant's pockets. They watched him take their money roll out and peel off a couple of bills and put the roll back in their pant's pockets. He hurried back to the wagon and climbed aboard and handed the money to the professor.

"Adios dear fellows; we hope to run across you again sometime when we can dazzle you with our many different talents and health remedies. Thank you for your patronage and your new clothes are right next to your old clothes," the professor called out as the wagons rattled on their way.

AJ and Brian stood silently watching as the wagons headed off to the south. Finally AJ looked at Brian and asked, "I wonder how much we paid for our new clothes?"

"I don't know, but I only had ten dollars on me. What about you?"

"I think I had twelve dollars."

Brian thought for a moment and then said with a grin, "The show the gals put on for us was worth the money."

AJ nodded in agreement as he scooped up some water and splashed it on his chest. After another long pause AJ said, "Do you think they'd come to the ranch and do a show for us?"

Brian looked at him with a serious look, "Do you think Pa would allow it?"

"No, but maybe we could send him to Dallas for some reason," AJ grinned.

"We'd still have Ma to contend with," Brian said thoughtfully.

"Forget it then," AJ said flatly.

**Raymond D. Mason**

# Chapter 6

**Pima County, Arizona**

**Jory Tatum** sat astraddle his horse atop a ridge that would give him a good view of the surrounding countryside. He rolled himself a cigarette as he waited for the men he was to meet. He stuck the cigarette between his lips and struck a match on the top of his saddle horn.

As he sat there he pondered the next few days and what they might mean to him. A minute or so later he saw a thin trail of dust in the distance and flipped the cigarette to the rocky ground.

Three men topped a hill to the south of where Tatum was waiting. The three men were led by a hired gun named Whitey Haisley, better known around as Whitey Howard. With Howard were Joe Carson and Pony Deal. Both men had wanted posters out on them.

Tatum rode down to meet the men, but looked around nervously as he rode for fear he'd overlooked a rider or two from the X-X ranch. The last people he wanted to be seen with by the other riders from the ranch were the three men he was about to meet.

When they rode up Whitey grinned widely, "Say kid, glad you showed up."

Jory snapped, "I said I'd be here; I am."

"Don't get your girdle in a knot; I was just making a comment. Now what is so all fired important that you'd call us away from three of the finest senoritas in all of Arizona to palaver," Whitey asked?

"I've got to make some money and get out of here. I heard that there's a shipment of silver going through here bound for Tucson. If we were to rob that stagecoach we'd all be set for a long time," Jory stated as he looked from one face to the next.

"Where'd you hear that at? I ain't heard no talk of any silver or gold shipments going through here, have you boys," Whitey asked the other two men with him?

Deal and Carson cast quick looks at Jory and shook their head no.

"Who told you about this shipment," Whitey asked suspiciously?

"It was just a guy I ran into. He seemed to know what he was talking about. He'd worked for the stage line, but got fired. I guess he wants to get back at them.

"He said the shipment was going through here tomorrow. I figure it's on the regular Tucson run. I know just the place where we could stop it. What do you say? Are you in...will you help me," Jory asked?

Whitey thought for a moment and then said, "Yeah, kid, we'll help you. But, there had better be silver or gold on that coach or you ain't going to like what'll happen to you."

"Hey, I'm just going by what this guy told me, Whitey. It wouldn't be my fault if he wasn't on the level with me," Jory said, his voice cracking slightly.

"Okay, we'll help you take care of the stagecoach, and you know what, kid; even if there isn't a silver or gold shipment I won't make you pay for it. If...that is, you'll do something for me in return. Either way though, kid, you'll come out ahead. If there is silver, or gold you win; and if there isn't silver or gold...and you do what I ask of you, you'll keep your life; so you win there too," Whitey said staring hard at Jory while wearing a twisted grin.

"Sure Whitey, anything for you. Just tell me what it is," Jory said quickly.

"I want you to set Lincoln Sackett up for me. That guy has cost me some good friends and I want his head. I'll tell you what I want you to do after we pull this stagecoach holdup," Whitey said with a sneer.

"Linc Sackett...why him," Jory asked nervously?

"I just told you, kid, he's cost me a couple of friends and I want to settle the score. In due time I'll tell you what to do, and, how to get him where I'll be waiting to kill him. You just do as you're told and we'll get along just fine," Whitey snapped.

Jory swallowed hard and slowly nodded his head in agreement. He had heard that Sackett was a hard man to bring down and the ones who had failed to do so paid for it with their lives.

Meanwhile, back at the X-X ranch house **Clay Butler** was having a rough time with a bronc he was busting. The horse did everything it could to lose its rider, but nothing worked and finally the horse gave up due to exhaustion.

"That was some good bronc busting, Clay," Buck Benton said with an approving grin.

"I'll tell you one thing, Buck; it probably looked a lot easier to you than it was for me. That little mare can flat out buck. I think she'll make a good saddle horse, though," Clay said as he started to take off his chaps.

"I'd leave those on for a little bit," Buck said and motioned towards another horse that was being saddled.

"Another one," Clay said and then chuckled. "I should have been a bookkeeper."

Just then Linc Sackett rode up to the corral where the bronc busting was taking place. He grinned when he saw Clay wearing the chaps and looking at the horse the men were attempting to saddle up.

"You're not going to put Clay on Tornado, are you? Not that killer," Linc said feigning concern?

Buck grinned knowing what Linc was doing. Clay looked at Linc and then quickly at Buck, "Is there something I should know about this Cayuse?"

"Just that he's a killer and is liable to get to twisting so bad he'll lift off the ground a couple of hundred feet, is all," Linc said holding his hands high above his head.

"It looks like I'd better pull my hat down a little tighter on my head, then," Clay said as he did just that.

"Hold that wild thing," Clay said once the other men had the saddle on it.

Clay climbed aboard and when the two men holding it by the ears let go, the horse just stood there kind of 'bowed up'. Clay waited, but nothing happened. He urged it to do something by giving it a kick with his boot heels. Nothing! He kicked it again, and still nothing.

When the horse sensed its rider had relaxed, it went straight up a good three feet and kicked wildly. The sudden bucking move caught Clay off guard and he sailed out of the saddle and found himself walking on thin air. He actually hit the ground on his feet, which was quite by accident.

Linc had started laughing when Clay left the saddle, but stopped in wonderment when Clay hit the ground standing and didn't fall.

"Well, I'll be...if that don't beat all," Linc said which brought a laugh from Buck and a wide grin from Clay.

"I don't believe it. How'd you manage that," Linc then asked Clay?

"When you're good, you're good, even when you get thrown," Clay replied.

"He got you there, Linc," Buck howled.

Before Clay had a chance to remount the horse, Buck saw two men riding down the road towards them.

"Now who is that? I hate to see strangers riding in; it usually spells trouble," Buck said to no one in particular.

The two men turned out to be another local rancher and his foreman. The rancher's name was Rudolph Hannigan and his foreman was Bob Ransom.

When they rode up to the corral Buck spoke, "Howdy Rudolph; I didn't recognize you and Bob. What brings you over this way?"

"I was wondering who you had working the southern end of your range land? Your cattle are all mixed in with mine. We found 'em when we went to do some branding this morning," Hannigan said in a serious tone.

"Dad gum it...I sent a kid we have working for us out there early this morning to round up any strays he found. Did you see anything of him," Buck frowned?

"Not a hair...What's this boy's name? If I see him I'll tell him about the strays," Hannigan offered.

"Jory Tatum; have you heard that name before," Buck asked curiously?

"Nope, can't say as I have. Well, I just thought I'd let you know," Hannigan said and started to rein his horse around when he spotted Clay Butler.

"Clay...Clay Butler, is that you," Hannigan asked in a surprised voice?

Clay looked over at Hannigan and frowned slightly. Hannigan noticed the perplexed look and responded.

"I bought a couple of fine horses from you about a year ago; the name's Hannigan," Hannigan said with a grin.

"Mr. Hannigan...well, I'll be. How are you? I forgot that you had a spread down here. As I remember your daughter was with you then. How is she doing," Clay asked politely?

"Oh, she's fine. She just got engaged to a young man she met on a trip into Tucson. Too bad, too; she was quite taken by you as I recall," Hannigan said with a laugh.

"Oh, really...I didn't know that," Clay said, actually a little embarrassed.

"You'll have to pay us a visit sometime. Buck can tell you how to get to our ranch when you want to ride over," Hannigan stated.

"Yes, I'll do that. The first chance I get, in fact," Clay said and looked at Buck.

"Well, you boys take it easy. We've got to get back now. I just wanted to let you know about those strays, Buck," Hannigan said as he and his foreman reined their horses around to ride off.

"Thanks, Rudolph, I'll take care of that little problem as soon as I can," Buck said.

As Hannigan and Ransom rode off, Buck said under his breath, "Now what has that kid been up to, anyway?"

*Raymond D. Mason*

# Chapter 7

**Jory Tatum** rode into the ranch yard and stopped at the corral. He had just climbed off his horse and was fixing to unsaddle it when he was approached by Buck Benton.

"Hold up there, Jory; I want to talk to you," Buck said in a stern voice.

"Yeah, what about," Jory said as he turned and gave his foreman a hard look?

"About your job on this ranch, for one thing," Buck snapped. "I told you to go and herd the strays from the south section of the ranch this morning. Mr. Hannigan just informed me that we have strays scattered all through his herd. What did you do all morning long," Buck asked with a deep frown?

"I herded strays back to our range, just like I was told. Don't start saying I ain't doing my job; I don't like it," Jory said belligerently.

"And I don't like someone being derelict in their duties. This is the second time you've failed to carry out my orders since you started here. Don't let it happen again," Buck said with a steady gaze at the young man.

"I don't need this job, Benton. I'm about to come into some money; a lot of money and I won't be herding this or any other bunch of cattle for anyone; anyone but myself, that is," Jory said boastfully.

"Oh, I see. You're going to get rich overnight, is that it? Well, that's good, but until then I'll expect you to do as you're told or ride on," Buck said.

"Is that an ultimatum, Buck?"

"It is if you're not planning on doing as you're told!"

Jory stood there for a moment and then turned and tightened the cinch on his saddle. Buck watched and wasn't the least bit surprised when Jory turned and stated, "Then I'll ride on."

With those words still hanging in the air, Jory stepped back upon his horse and rode away. Buck watched him go, but turned and looked at Linc Sackett when he heard his voice behind him.

"Where's Jory going?"

Buck shook his head, "Who knows? Wherever it is, it won't be on this ranch. He just quit."

"Quit? Not over that little card game incident last night," Linc asked?

"No, no...that boy's got some problems that only Jory Tatum can deal with. I just hope he gets his head squared away before he gets himself in big trouble.

## Sackett Ranch

**John Sackett** sat in his small office just off the ranch house living room going over a list of items they would need from town. He heard some loud shouting coming from the front of the house and got up to see what all the commotion was about.

John walked through the living room to the front door and saw that three of his ranch hands were in a heated argument about something. He quickly recognized the men as Snake Eyes Bob, and Rawhide Deacon. They were both yelling at one of his top hands by the name of Wayne Miles.

"You said I could have your saddle when you got enough money saved up to buy a new one," Rawhide said angrily.

"I didn't say I'd give it to you, Deacon, I said I'd sell it to you," Wayne said.

"I heard him too, Deacon; he said he'd give it to you," Snake Eyes Bob said, siding with his partner.

With their backs turned towards the house they didn't see John Sackett approaching them. When he spoke, however, both men wheeled around in surprise.

"I heard him, and Wayne said he'd sell you his saddle, Deacon," John said, having been present when Wayne had made the statement.

"Howdy, John...we didn't know you was there. You're wrong, though, Wayne said he'd give me the saddle and now he wants to charge me for it," Deacon argued.

"John, I told Deacon just now that I'd sell him that saddle for twenty dollars. It's worth every bit of forty, forty five dollars, but he wants it for nothing," Wayne argued in his own defense.

"I know Wayne, I heard you when you told him that. Now if you want the saddle, Deacon, cough

51

up the twenty dollars. If not, then drop the subject all together," John said firmly.

Deacon looked angrily at John and then gave Snake Eyes Bob a quick look.

"Come on, Bob; they're working against us," Deacon said.

"No one is working against you, Deacon; that was the deal," John said, hoping to put an end to the argument.

"I'll tell you one thing, John, I don't like being called a liar and that's what you're doing...calling me a liar," Deacon said through gritted teeth.

John's eyes narrowed to mere slits as he said slowly, "You're looking for trouble, Deacon. Something's been eating at you for several weeks now, so whatever it is lay it out here right now and let's deal with it."

"All right, I'll tell you what it is. When my woman came out here from town last month you put your arm around her in such a way that it made my blood boil. I didn't say anything at the time, but the more I thought about it, the madder I got," Deacon said tightly.

John looked shocked at the man's claim.

"Deacon, I've known Sally for years; she's like a sister to me, if anything. The way I put my arm around her is the way I hug my daughter, my sisters, my God man, even the preacher's wife. It's certainly nothing to get upset about," John argued.

"No man should hug another man's woman the way you did; pulling her up to your side like that," Deacon went on.

"If I'd been making a play for her, the hug would have been from the front, don't you think," John said and then paused before adding.

"Sally didn't think anything was out of line at the time. I remember how we were laughing and joking when she got in the buggy to leave."

"Well, she wants nothing to do with you now, I can tell you that," Deacon groused.

"Obviously you had something to do with it then. Everyone knows you do the thinking for her," John said with a deep set frown and then went on.

"Something else has your cinch in a knot, Deacon; what is it?"

"Alright, I'll tell you. You took sides in a poker game awhile back when I dropped a card by accident off the table. You said the card was dead; I said it wasn't because when it fell it landed face down. That hand cost me a weeks pay and you caused it," Deacon snapped.

"I thought so. You'd make up something rather than deal with what it was that was really bothering you. You're a dishonest man, Deacon. Maybe it's time you and Snake Eyes look for employment somewhere else," John said flatly.

"You mean you're firing us," Deacon said, his face and neck reddening slightly?

John replied with his own affirmative head nod.

"Come on Bob; let's go somewhere where the air is fresher smelling," Deacon said.

The two turned to go but paused for a moment before Deacon spun around, pulling his gun in the process, and firing two bullets. The first one hit

53

John Sackett in the side; the second one hit Wayne in the chest.

Both men went to the ground. Snake Eyes Bob pulled his gun and put another slug into Wayne before shouts from the barn and corral area called out. The two men made a mad dash for their horses; swung into the saddles and rode away at a full run.

Several of the hired hands rushed to where the two men had fallen and began to work over them. They saw that Wayne was dead, but John Sackett was still alive.

"Let's get John into the house," one of the hired hands said and he and another cowhand picked John up and carried him into the ranch house.

"Did anyone see who it was who did this," someone asked?

"Rawhide Deacon and Snake Eyes Bob; I saw the whole thing," one of the men said.

John was still conscious and nodded his head when asked it was those two who had shot Wayne and him. The men looked at one another knowing what AJ and Brian would do once they got word of the shootings.

Dusty Collier, one of the hired hands turned to another and said under his breath, "I'd hate to be in Deacon and Bob's place. There won't be anyplace they'll be able to hide from them two boys of John's."

# Chapter 8

**Brian Sackett** gave **AJ** a serious look and said through half clenched teeth, "Looks like another chase is in order. I'll follow those two to China if I have to. They'll pay for this with their lives."

"You're not going alone this time, Brian. I'll be going with you. Dusty can run the ranch while we're gone. Hopefully it won't take us long to catch up to these two no-goods," AJ stated.

"I want to get an early start before their trail gets cold. Knowing those two they'll head south. I remember Deacon talking about a brother who lives in San Felipe del Rio, down on the Mexican border. I hope we can catch up to 'em before they get there. Otherwise we may be spending some time in Mexico," Brian said.

"We've got daylight left. We can be ready to leave inside an hour," AJ said with a deep frown.

"It won't take me that long to be ready to ride," Brian replied.

Within the hour the two brothers had mounted up, and leading a pack horse, headed south in the direction they figured the two men would be going. They hoped they could catch up to Rawhide Deacon and Snake Eyes Bob before they got too far from the Sackett ranch. That, however, was more wishful thinking than anything else.

They picked up what they believed to be Deacon and Bob's trail about a mile from the ranch house and noticed that one of the horse's shoes had a slight crack in it that would make it easier to follow.

Due to the fact that it was late in the day, the brothers figured on riding until just before dark and then making camp. Hopefully the two men they were pursuing wouldn't plan on someone being on their trail so soon after the shooting and ride at a slower pace.

When it got too dark to follow the horse's tracks, the brothers made camp for the night. They knew now that it might take them a couple of days to catch up to Deacon and Bob. They'd get a decent night's rest and hit the trail at dawn's first light.

On the second day out, with the sun just sinking in the West, Brian and AJ topped a hill that gave them a good view of the surrounding terrain. Off in the distance Brian caught sight of two riders heading south. He reined up and motioned for AJ to stop also.

"Look over there, AJ; doesn't that look like Deacon and Bob?"

"I'd say so. How far do you think they are ahead of us?"

"Maybe a mile and a half," Brian estimated.

"If they see us the race will be on; and with it getting so late in the day we could lose them in the dark," AJ said as he stood up in the stirrups to give his back a rest.

"What are you saying? We should stay behind them and not make our move until morning?"

"No, we'll keep an eye on them and see if it looks like they're going to make camp. As I recall there's a stream not too far from here and I think that's where they'll stop."

"Oh, I see. Let 'em make camp and move up and take 'em then, is that it," Brian asked?

"It'll be a lot harder for them to see us if they're in the campfire's light and we're out of it. If they decide to make a fight of it the advantage is definitely in our favor."

"You're right there. If we stay off the ridges they might not see us. We'll stay just high enough to see where they make camp. Let's head that way," Brian said motioning along a low lying hill top that would still allow them a good view.

Brian and AJ had been able to see where the two men they were following made camp. With the night being black due to just a sliver of the moon it definitely worked in the Sackett's favor. Deacon and Snake Eyes had camped alongside a creek that also worked in the brother's favor. The sound of the rippling water would cover the sound of their movement.

Deacon tossed another small branch on the campfire and told Snake Eyes he was going to get some shuteye. Bob told Deacon he wanted to check on the horses and then he would be turning in also.

Brian and AJ waited in the darkness no more than five feet beyond the campfire's light.

Bob returned after checking to make sure the horses were securely tied and he too lay down. AJ and Brian looked at one another and grinned. All they had to do now was give the two men a few minutes to get to sleep and they would be able to take them easily.

They had waited about three minutes when Brian suddenly tensed and looked to his right. Due to the darkness he could not make out what he'd seen, but there was definitely something, or someone, quietly moving around. AJ also heard something, but to his left.

The breaking of a twig on the opposite side of the campsite caused Snake Eyes Bob to sit upright and draw his gun. That was all it took for the small Comanche war party to let out a blood curdling scream and attack.

Snake Eyes began firing at the Indians as did Deacon once he was alerted. Brian and AJ looked at one another in disbelief. They had to make a quick decision as to whether they should help Deacon and Bob fight off the attacking Indians, or let the Comanche war party do the work they had set out to do. The decision was made for them when two Comanche warriors jumped them from behind.

The splashing of the water behind Brian alerted him to the attacking warrior and he whirled around just in time to catch the brave in mid air and grabbing the Indian's arm that held the knife. They both fell to the ground in a struggle to the death.

AJ was also jumped and took a slight knife wound to the shoulder. He was able to get a shot off, however, that hit the attacking Comanche in the stomach. AJ then turned and fired at the Indian who was atop of Brian, killing him.

When the other Indians heard the gunfire coming from outside the camp, they turned their attention towards it. They began firing in the direction of Brian and AJ causing the brothers to take cover.

With the Comanche warriors preoccupied with the Sackett brothers, Deacon and Snake Eyes were able to scramble to their horses and make a clean getaway. They didn't know for sure who it was that had diverted the Indian's attention, but they had a good idea.

There were a total of nine Comanche braves had been involved in the attack. AJ had killed two of them, while Snake Eyes and Deacon had killed three. The other four escaped into the darkness.

Brian and AJ stayed there the rest of the night; Brian tending to AJ's knife wound. The next morning they managed to pick up the trail of Deacon and Snake Eyes once again. They were still headed south.

**Raymond D. Mason**

# Chapter 9

**270 Miles S/E of
Santa FE, New Mexico**

**Brent** told **Julia** he was going to ride up to the lead wagon and talk to the major. For sometime he had been having second thoughts about going north to Santa Fe when they could go on a straighter route to Los Angeles via the Southern Emigrant Trail, but had not expressed his concerns to Julia or Grant.

Brent had heard that the California Trail was a very rough route and that the Old Spanish Trail was even rougher. If that was the case, why had the major chosen that particular route? Brent wanted an answer.

The major looked over at Brent when he rode up alongside his wagon and nodded, "What do ya say, Johnson," the major asked?

"Major...I'd like to know what you've learned about the Old Spanish Trail and this California Trail connection that makes you think it's the best route to take to the Sacramento Valley. I've heard that both routes are very rough for wagons," Brent said, coming straight to the point.

The major gave Brent a hard stare before saying, "I have a map that takes a slightly different route around the toughest spots on both trails."

"I'd like to see that map if I could," Brent replied.

"What's the matter, Johnson; don't you trust me," the major questioned.

"It's not that so much, as, I'm just naturally curious. I've talked to a number of people who told me those trails are very rough going. If you know another route and you've got a map, I'd like to see it."

"No one else on the train has questioned my decision. Why are you?"

"I have a woman who is expecting a baby and she's tending to an infant now. I don't want to make the trip any harder for her than need be," Brent said firmly.

"You should have thought about that before you joined up with us. I'm not about to change the route we're taking because of your concern. If you don't like the idea then you can always take another trail but we're going to Santa Fe," the major stated firmly.

"I'm thinking of doing just that. I appreciate you allowing us to join up with you, but we'll be leaving you and heading for Las Cruces and the Southern Route."

"So be it then," the major said unconcerned.

Brent reined his horse around and rode back to the rear of the wagon train where their wagon was located.

*Five Faces West*

"What did you want to talk to the major about," Julia asked?

"I told him that we won't be going with them to Santa Fe. We're going to Las Cruces and pick up the Southern Emigrant Trail," Brent said with a slight smile.

"Oh...is there a reason you don't want to stay with this wagon train," Julia questioned.

"Yeah, there is. I've heard it's not a good route. We'll hook up with another wagon train that's headed west," Brent said with confidence.

Julia didn't argue, but couldn't help but wonder about Brent's decision. She had met several of the women on the wagon train and had struck up good acquaintances with them. But, if Brent thought it would be better to take up with a different train, so be it.

Grant had been riding ahead of the wagon train with the scout, Jim Bowers. After Brent had tethered his saddle horse to the rear of the wagon and had taken the harness reins again, Grant rode up.

"Brent, I just heard the major tell Bowers that we'll be leaving the wagon train...is that right?"

"Yeah, Grant, when they turn north for Santa Fe."

"Jim was telling me that the major knows a way that is a lot easier than the other routes. He said we'd be making a mistake leaving them."

"I don't think so, Grant. There's something about this whole idea that doesn't sit right with me."

"The major's afraid that our leaving might start the others to thinking about doing the same thing.

63

Him and Bowers are pretty upset," Grant said raising his eyebrows for effect.

"That's their problem, not ours," Brent said evenly.

"I think they're going to bring it up tonight when we make camp," Grant said.

"That's fine with me, Grant. If they put me on the spot I'll tell the entire wagon train why we're leaving and a few of them might want to join us."

"I know the major wouldn't like that."

"Then he'd best not bring it up," Brent said with finality in his voice.

Sure enough, that night while everyone was sitting around the big campfire, the major got everyone's attention.

"Excuse me folks, but I want you to hear this from me and not through the rumor mill. We'll be losing the Johnson wagon tomorrow. It seems they don't want to go on the route we're taking, but would rather risk the bandits and Apache Indians on the southern route," the major said.

Everyone seated around the campfire looked in Brent, Julia, and Grant's direction. There was a murmur went up as folks made comments to one another.

"I say good riddance," Jacob Dean called out.

Brent gave the man a quick, angry look. This wasn't the first time Dean had made snide remarks at these gatherings.

"The route we're taking is the safest, and the easiest route you can take to the Sacramento Valley area. I think the Johnson's are planning on going to Los Angeles. Ain't that right, Brent," the major stated.

"Yeah, that's right, and then we'll take the El Camino Real north to San Francisco," Brent answered calmly.

"What did you join up with us for in the first place, Johnson," Dean snapped.

Brent frowned deeply as he said, "We didn't know where you were headed when we joined you. Since we were heading west, traveling with a wagon train seemed a lot safer than traveling alone."

"What if you can't find a wagon train going on out to California? Are you going to go on by yourself from Las Cruces," Dean asked?

"If we have to Dean...yes," Brent answered.

"Well, like I said...good riddance."

Brent's jaws tightened as he held his tongue. Julia looked at him and could see that Dean was pushing him a little too much. Finally Brent had to say something in response to the rudeness Dean was exhibiting.

"The main reason we're leaving the train, Dean, is because of the stench we have to breathe that's coming from your wagon," Brent stated in a taut tone of voice.

There was total silence in the camp as heads turned and looked at Jacob Dean. His face reddened and a vein stood out down the middle of his forehead.

"A man could get hurt making a statement like that Johnson," Dean said through clenched teeth.

"You've been on my case since the day we joined up with this wagon train, Dean. I've watched you bully some of the folks around and I'm tired of you and your mouth. Now I'm calling you out...put up or shut up," Brent said with a scowl on his face.

"Hold it right there," the major said. "There'll be no fighting between the two of you on this train. Now I want you two to knock it off."

Brent looked at the major and then at Dean. After a couple of silent seconds he said to Julia, "Come on, let's go back to our wagon."

They got up and started back to where their wagon was, but had to pass by Dean. Just as they got even with him, Dean said under his breath, "Stench, huh," and took a swing at Brent.

Brent blocked the punch and hit Dean a hard right to the stomach. Dean let out a loud gasp as he doubled over with his eyes bugging out due to having the breath knocked out of him. Brent looked at him and then turned back to the others and said, "Goodnight, folks," and he and Julia, followed by Grant went back to their wagon.

# Chapter 10

**Pima County,
Arizona Territory**

**Jory Tatum** along with Whitey Howard, Joe Carson, and Pony Deal waited for the stage bound for Tucson. Jory was nervous which got Whitey's attention. He grinned at the young man and said, "Calm down, Jory; it's only a stagecoach."

"This is the first one I've ever robbed, though," Jory said truthfully.

Whitey laughed, "Why, I thought you were an old hand at this, boy. So you're a virgin highwayman, huh."

Jory cast a quick look towards Whitey and saw Deal and Carson also grinning. He hoped the coach was carrying some kind of payload on it. He'd made up the story about the man telling him the stagecoach would be carrying silver. All he really wanted was to get enough money so he could get out of Arizona and go to California.

"Here it comes, boys," Whitey said and pulled his bandana up over his nose.

The other's covered their faces as well and waited for the coach to draw near. Jory was glad to see there was a man riding shotgun, because that meant there might be something of value on the coach.

The four of them rode out from behind the rocks and blocked the road so the coach had to stop. With guns drawn and aimed at the guard and driver Whitey called out, "Hold up there. Don't do anything stupid."

The guard had the thought to try to get a shot off from his double barreled shotgun, but with four holdup men facing them decided against it.

"Throw down your guns and then the strongbox," Whitey ordered.

Just then, a man inside the stagecoach leaned out and fired his six-shooter at the bandits. He missed them, but incurred the wrath of Pony Deal and Joe Carson who rode up alongside the coach and began firing through the windows.

They wounded a woman and killed the man who'd fired at them. When the guard went for his rifle in the coach's boot well, Whitey Howard shot and wounded him as well.

"Now throw down that strongbox and be quick about it," Whitey ordered.

The driver threw down the box and Whitey told him to get out of there and make it quick. The driver wasted no time in doing just that. Once the coach disappeared over a hill, the men quickly opened up the strongbox.

Whitey looked inside the box and then looked at Jory Tatum. He grinned as he said, "It looks like we've struck pay dirt, men. There must be over a thousand dollars here. Of course, it ain't no silver shipment."

"How much is there, Whitey," Pony Deal asked?

"Let's see, one, two, three...," Whitely counted until he'd counted it all out.

"I make it to be eleven hundred and twenty dollars. That makes it three hundred a piece for us and two hundred and twenty for Jory," Whitey said with a half grin.

Jory looked quickly at Whitey and then at the grinning faces of the other two men. He wasn't going to argue. Two hundred and twenty dollars was two hundred and fifteen dollars more than he had in his pockets right then.

"Give me my money and let's get out of here," Jory said still nervous.

"Simmer down, son. In due time; in due time...but, you still have a favor to do for me, remember?"

Jory looked quickly at Whitey and then said, "Favor?"

"Now don't tell me you forgot, Jory. You're going to set Linc Sackett up for me, remember. If you don't do it...you ain't leaving here alive," Whitey said with his half grin.

"Oh, yeah...I forgot. Okay, Whitey, when do you want me to do this and how," Jory asked quickly?

Jory had not told Whitey that he had quit the ranch the day before out of fear of the man. He knew that Whitey wouldn't hesitate killing him if he crossed him. His plan was to be as far away

**Raymond D. Mason**

from this area as he could come sunup the next morning.

"I want it done tomorrow morning. I'll give you the details as to how you're to go about it at Muldoon's. Now come on, let's get out of here before someone comes along," Whitey said as he shoved the money they'd stolen into his saddlebags.

When they arrived at Muldoon's the four of them went inside and divvied up the money; Jory getting his two hundred and twenty and the others taking three hundred each.

Whitey went over the details of how Jory was to get Linc Sackett out to the spot he'd chosen to ambush him. Jory listened intently and when Whitey had finished, agreed to doing it, saying it shouldn't be any problem in pulling it off.

"Now I want you to go back out to the X-X and tell Linc that you found some of their cattle in a small sealed off area in Mule Canyon. By the time you and him get out there, we'll be ready."

"What if he wants to bring others from the ranch with us," Jory asked?

"Let 'em come; the more the merrier, that's what I always say," Whitey said with a high pitched laugh.

Jory sat there for a moment and when he got a questioning look from Whitey said, "What?"

"What are you waiting for, boy?"

"You mean you want it done today," Jory asked in surprise?

"Yea, today...what did you think; the next 4$^{th}$ of July or something," Whitey snapped, the smile dropping from his face.

"I thought you meant tomorrow morning. It's kind of late in the day for him to want to ride all the way out to Mule Canyon. That's a good forty mile round trip from the ranch," Jory argued.

Whitey looked at the young man and then pulled a pocket watch from his vest pocket. He nodded his head for a moment and then said, "Okay, tomorrow morning. You have him on the way out there by six o'clock in the morning though...do you hear me."

"Okay, Whitey; by six o'clock," Jory agreed.

"Now let's drink up," Whitey grinned and then called to one of the three women in the small makeshift saloon, "Come over here, ladies. It's time to have some fun."

Jory Tatum had saddled up and was on his way to Tucson before the sun came up the next morning. He had a good feeling about leaving Arizona. He believed his future lay in the San Francisco area or maybe Sacramento.

Tatum topped a hill and looked back to make sure he wasn't being followed. Assured that he wasn't, he urged his horse on down the gentle slope. He was about a hundred yards from a small dry creek when Whitey Howard rode out from behind a large rock.

Tatum pulled his horse to a halt and his eyes widened with fear. He reined his horse to the left and started to kick it into a run, but Pony Deal rode out from behind a small thicket of buck brush.

Kicking his horse into a full run, Tatum headed in the only direction he felt was left open to him.

Howard and Deal gave chase as Tatum spurred his horse on. He was looking over his shoulder and didn't see Joe Carson ride out from behind a stand of Palo Verde trees.

Carson took careful aim at the approaching Tatum and squeezed the Winchester's trigger. The gun bucked and a split second later Tatum did a backward somersault off his horse. The bullet had hit the young man in the right shoulder, but with enough force to send him off his horse backwards.

The three men rode up to where Tatum lay. He looked up at them with fear and pain in his eyes. His eyes darted from one man to the next. Each of the men looked down at him with expressionless stares on their face.

Finally Whitey Howard shook his head negatively and very slowly as he aimed his pistol at Jory.

"You are not long for this world, kid. Adios," Howard said and squeezed the trigger.

The bullet hit Tatum squarely between the eyes. Pony Deal cocked his pistol and fired a bullet into the young man's chest. Since Joe Carson had been the one to bring him off his horse, he didn't shoot the now dead man.

"Let's go," Howard said. "I'll take care of Linc Sackett next. Let's pay him a visit at the X-X."

# Chapter 11

**Carlsbad, New Mexico**

**Brent Sackett** reined their wagon to the front of a general store and pulled to a stop. He looked at Julia and smiled. Julia handed little Gracie over to Brent while she climbed down out of the wagon. Once she was on the ground Brent handed the baby to her.

"While you're picking up what we need Julia, Grant and I are going to grab a quick beer," Brent said as he jumped to the ground.

"Just one, Brent...promise me," Julia said with a half pleading look on her face.

"Uh, maybe two...you know a man can't walk on one leg," Brent grinned.

Julia laughed, "Okay, two then."

Julia headed into the general store and Brent and Grant headed for the nearest saloon. They found one about five buildings down from the general store, went in and bellied up to the bar next to two Mexican men dressed like caballeros. One of the men was Santos Barela, a New Mexico bandit with a price on his head.

Barela looked at the two men who had 'sided' him and frowned. Brent gave him a glance and then a second look. The two men glared at one another for a moment and then both looked away.

Brent certainly wasn't looking for trouble and Barela didn't want to draw attention to the fact that he was in town. The man standing next to Barela was another notorious man on the dodge by the name of Santos Benavides. Both men were hot tempered and hated 'Gringos'.

"What'll it be gents," the bartender asked?

"Two beers," Brent said and looked at Grant. "These are going to go down real easy, kid."

The bartender drew the beer and set the mugs in front of Brent and Grant.

"Ten cents," he said.

Brent tossed two nickels onto the bar and one of them rolled over near Barela's hand. The Mexican instantly put his finger on the coin, but a noise behind Brent and Grant caused them to look back and neither saw what Barela had done.

The bartender waited for a moment and then repeated, "I need ten cents."

"I gave you two nickels," Brent replied.

"I only see one nickel," the bartender said even though he had seen Barela take the nickel.

"I put it right there," Brent said pointing where the coin had hit the bar.

"Hey, Hombre...we do not like for a stranger to try and get a beer without paying," Barela said, giving Brent a hard look.

"I don't really care what you like...Hombre. I put two nickels on this bar and only one is there now; so either you or this bartender took the other one. My guess is...it's you," Brent said coldly.

Barela looked at Brent for a second and then gave Benavides a glance before saying, "You're calling me a thief?"

"If the name applies I guess I am," Brent said moving his hand to the gun on his hip.

"Forget it, stranger. I'll give you a beer," the bartender said.

"No, you won't. I want the one who has the nickel to show it," Brent said.

Grant looked around at the rest of the barroom and saw that the majority of patrons were Mexican. There were a few Anglos in the room, but only five others.

Just then the barroom doors opened and a man entered and gave the two Mexicans a hard stare. The man's name was **Pat Garrett**; he was just passing through on his way to Lincoln County, but was well known to the two badmen. He walked up and stood next to Grant at the bar.

"Give me a beer," Garrett said.

Slowly Barela moved his hand from over the nickel. Brent looked at the nickel and then gave Barela a quick glance. Barela turned his face away so Ascarate couldn't see it. He nudged Benavides and the two of them drank up and walked to the door of the bar.

When Barela and Benavides reached the doorway, Barela looked back at Brent and aimed at him; using his finger as though it was a pistol. Brent merely grinned.

Once he and Grant had drank down their two beers, they went back to the general store to meet Julia. She had gathered together the things they were in need of and was ready to go.

"You're sure you have everything," Brent asked?

"Yes, I wanted a couple of things for little Gracie; and a few things for the trip, of course."

"Of course," Brent grinned.

"Oh, Grant, the women in the store said she was the cutest thing they'd ever seen," Julia said with a smile.

"She is ain't she," Grant said proudly.

Brent was listening to this and was wearing a slight grin until he looked down the street and saw the two Mexican men he'd had the encounter with in the saloon. They were both watching him.

When Brent locked onto them with his gaze Barela laughed and the two of them turned and walked on down the street. Brent watched them and then looked back at Julia.

"I'll have to check around and see if anyone knows of any wagon trains coming through here. If there aren't we'll have to go on by ourselves. Are you up to it," Brent asked in a concerned voice?

Julia smiled, "Yes, Brent; I'll make it just fine."

"Well, I'd better find out where we can camp for the night," Brent stated. "I'm sure there's someplace close to town," he added.

They climbed aboard the wagon and headed on down the street. When they got to the livery stable Brent pulled the wagon to a halt and jumped down.

"I'll ask the guy in here if he knows of any wagon trains due in town. Usually they're one of the first to find out. I'll be right back."

Brent went inside the stable office and asked the owner if he'd heard of any wagon trains headed that way. The stable owner told him he had not heard of any, but if he wanted to wait around he could camp out right there at the livery stable and just pay for the up keep of the horses.

Brent thanked the man and explained that they'd only be staying the one night. The man told Brent to go down the street to the Land Office and he could pick up a map of the Southern Emigrant Trail and where the waterholes were; or at least had been. Brent thanked him and went back out and told Julia and Grant what he'd learned.

They parked the wagon out of the way and put the horses up for the night. Brent asked Grant to wait there with Julia while he went to see about picking up a map. He was able to get one from the clerk with no trouble; but the man did give him a word of advice. Watch for bandits and renegade Apache war parties.

The next morning, bright and early, they were on the trail to California once again; this time, however, traveling without the company of an entire wagon train.

**Raymond D. Mason**

# Chapter 12

**Paint Rock, Texas**

**Brian** and **AJ** picked up the trail of Deacon and Snake Eyes early the next morning and could tell the two men were pushing their horses a lot harder than before. Now that the two desperadoes knew they had someone on their trail they weren't about to take their time getting to Deacon's brother's place near the Mexican border.

AJ leaned out of the saddle as he checked the horseshoe tracks made by Deacon and Bob's horses. He looked back in the direction they'd just come from and then looked off into the distance.

"What's eatin' you, AJ," Brian asked, noticing AJ's actions?

"Deacon and Bob are riding like they're drunk. They're weaving their way south. I guess they're doing anything in their power to try and lose us. Look at these tracks."

Brian leaned out of the saddle and checked the ground also. He looked back up the hill they'd just came down and then looked at the hill off to the right of it. It was true. Deacon and Bob were zigzagging their way to his brother's place; if that was where they were going.

"Now why do you think they're doing that," Brian asked?

"I think they want to find some hard ground that will force us to slow down. It's my guess they're headed to San Felipe del Rio and hoping to lose us. Hey, those two don't have any more brains than a longhorn steer does, you know," AJ replied.

When they reached a point where the ground was quite a bit harder Brian caught sight of something that he instantly called to AJ's attention.

"AJ, look at this. That's drops of blood. Either Deacon or Bob is bleeding. He must have been wounded in the scuffle with the Comanche's last night," Brian said.

"It looks that way, all right. That little fact alone could slow them down considerable. Depending on which one it is who is wounded, that is. If it's Deacon who is wounded we may find his body alongside the trail. Snake Eyes Bob wouldn't hesitate in killing him," AJ said seriously.

"Why don't we just ride a straight line to del Rio? If that's where they're going we can be there waiting for them when they arrive," Brian wondered aloud.

"I don't know what Deacon's brother's name is, do you? We'd have no way of locating the man if Deacon isn't known around town. No, we'll keep tracking them. Besides, they may not be going to Deacon's brother's place down there. It's just a guess on my part," AJ answered.

AJ looked at Brian and then turned his attention towards the ridge of a hill parallel to them. Riding in the same direction as them were five Comanche Indians. AJ pointed in the Indian's direction and called to Brian.

"Speaking of pushing horses harder, little brother, I think we'd be wise to do the same thing."

Brian looked in the direction of the Indians and the two of them kicked their horses into full gallops; kicking up a trail of dust as they rode hard, down the gentle slope. The Comanche's did the same. AJ was slightly ahead and saw that they could put a little more distance between themselves and the Indians if they veered to their left at the bottom of the hill.

When the Comanche's reached the bottom of the hill they were on, they continued straight and rode across a small stream and up the bank on the other side. AJ and Brian had turned to their left and were still burning leather as they followed the stream.

They rounded the first bend and reined to a quick stop. They were faced with a steep hill that was mostly rock. There was no place for them to go. The only way the two could go was back in the direction from which they'd come.

"Bad move," AJ said.

"We could make a stand right here," Brian stated.

"I don't think we'd last long. Not with those Comanche up there shooting down at us. It'd be like shooting fish in a barrel...and we'd be the fish."

"Then we'll make a fight of it from horseback," Brian said pulling his rifle from its scabbard.

"Now you're talking," AJ replied and did the same.

They reined their horses around and rode back in the direction they'd come holding their rifles in one hand, but ready for action. They kept expecting to run into the Indians, but nothing happened.

When they reached the spot where they had made their turn, they reined up. There was no sign of the Indians anywhere. They looked around nervously, waiting for all hell to break loose at any moment. Nothing happened.

"What do you make of this," AJ asked in a puzzled tone of voice?

"Hey, your guess is as good as mine," Brian replied.

"Did you see which direction they went," AJ questioned.

"No, I was too busy waiting for bullets to start flying. Those warriors were carrying repeating rifles," Brian said.

"I noticed that too. Now when did the Indian Affairs boys start issuing repeaters to the Comanche," AJ answered.

Noise dead ahead of them caused both men to raise their rifles and cock the hammers back. They waited for the Comanche's to show them selves, but they never did. Instead eight Texas Rangers came riding around the bend of the small stream.

Both Sackett brothers raised their rifles high over their head to show the rangers they meant no harm. The rangers returned the gesture and continued to ride in the brothers' direction.

"Man, are we glad to see you fellas," AJ said.

"Oh, why's that," the lead ranger asked?

"A Comanche war party coming down that ridge over there is why. We had a run in with a small party last night and then we see this one today, they must have been going to join up," AJ stated.

"We've had reports of several attacks in the area. You boys were lucky we happened along. Which way did the Comanche's go?"

AJ pointed on the other side of the stream and said, "They must have gone straight on across the creek. We headed that way," he said, pointing up stream, "but ran into a box canyon. What brings you men out here?"

"We're tracking a gang who robbed a Wells Fargo freight office and shot one of the clerks. You ain't seen three men riding like Old Joe was after them, have you," the leader of the rangers asked?

"No, the only ones we've seen are the Comanche's we've had run-ins with. You didn't meet two men headed south by any chance did you," AJ asked?

"We did at that. They looked like they were in a hurry to get from somewhere or to somewhere by the way they were riding. You wouldn't be after them, would you?"

"Yeah, we are. They shot our pa and lit out. We're planning on taking them back to stand trial," AJ stated.

One of the rangers, Reuben Boyce, had been eyeing Brian with a studious eye. He wore a frown that illustrated he was deep in thought. Suddenly he whipped out his pistol and aimed it at Brian.

"Hold it right there, Sackett," Boyce snapped.

The ranger in charge, Captain John Barclay Armstrong, looked around quickly and asked, "What are you doing Reuben?"

"This is Brent Sackett, John. He's wanted for shootin' the sheriff of Crystal City and some other small town sheriff. I was just reading the poster on him the other day," Boyce stated.

"You've got the Sackett name right but I'm not Brent. I'm his twin brother, Brian. This is our older brother, AJ," Brian explained.

"Did that paper say anything about Sackett having a twin brother, Reuben," Armstrong asked?

"Not a word."

"Well, it looks like we'll have to take you in until we can get this all cleared up," Armstrong said.

"Ranger, he's telling the truth. If you'll contact any lawman in Shackelford or Taylor counties they'll clear this whole thing up. We have a large ranch up that way," AJ said in a firm, almost angry tone of voice.

"We can't very well do that out here in the middle of nowhere, now can we," Armstrong stated and then went on. "Reuben, you caught him, you take the two of them back to headquarters and check his claim out."

"I'd better give him a hand, Captain," one of the other rangers said.

"Ed, you've been looking for more excuses to leave us; what's the matter have you got a hot date with some senorita or something," the captain snapped. "Well, go ahead and give Reuben a hand."

"Thanks, Captain," Ed said.

"Better take their guns," the captain said.

Although the two brothers protested it was to no avail. The rangers took their pistols and rifles and handcuffed them with their hands in front of them so they could still hold onto their saddle horns for mounting and dismounting.

"You can just wait there for us once you get this whole thing squared away with these boys," Armstrong ordered.

The Sackett brothers started riding ahead of the rangers knowing they were losing valuable time in catching up to Deacon and Snake Eyes Bob. The four riders had only ridden about a hundred yards when the first gunshots rang out. The shots weren't fired at them, however, but at the other six rangers behind them.

Instantly the two rangers whirled around to see where the gunshots were coming from. When they did, Brian looked at AJ and the two of them kicked their horses into a full run down the stream.

The ranger named Ed looked in the direction of the fleeing Sackett's, but quickly returned his attention to the gunshots. Ranger Boyce never gave the brothers a second thought. He headed back in the direction of the other rangers. When Ed saw Boyce returning to help the other rangers, he reacted, also; he headed in the opposite direction.

The rangers under attack took cover and started firing back at the Comanche's. The war party had seen the approaching rangers earlier and took cover until the proper moment to attack. Their attack had actually worked in AJ and Brian's favor.

The Sackett boys rode hard along the stream until they reached a good place to cross it and head south. They both had to deal with having their hands cuffed, but at least they were free.

As they rode hard down the hillside Brian glanced back to see if the rangers were pursuing them. The rangers weren't giving chase, but three Comanche warriors were. The race was on.

# Chapter 13

**Pima County,
Arizona Territory**

**Linc Sackett** climbed aboard the buckboard and reined the team in the direction of the main road. He was on his way to Tucson to escort Miss Shauna back to the ranch. She had taken a stagecoach to Prescott to visit an aunt and uncle who lived there. Buck normally would have picked Miss Shauna up, but he told Linc he would be busy with a cattle deal and wanted him to do the honors.

The trip to Tucson and back would take two full days, so Linc left the ranch early in the morning. He almost felt guilty at being able to do something that was as easy as merely fetching Miss Shauna from Tucson.

Linc had traveled about four miles from the ranch and was enjoying the ride, when he saw two riders atop a ridge off to his left. He watched the men and determined that they were heading in the same direction as him.

He couldn't help but wonder why they didn't take the stagecoach road since it would be much easier travel than riding the ridges. Perhaps they felt they could see the surrounding terrain better. Whatever their reason, Linc kept an eye on them.

After having traveled another couple of miles Linc came to a small creek and stopped to let the team of horses drink. When he looked back in the direction of the two riders, they had disappeared from the ridge. He quickly scoured the hills on both sides of the road, but they were no where to be seen.

With this area being well known for stagecoach holdups, Linc hoped the men weren't road agents taking him for a well heeled rancher. The surprise would be on them if that were the case.

He let the horses drink their fill and then moved on up the road. He actually felt better when he saw the two men reappear atop another ridge farther up ahead. It appeared they had stopped when he had, to let the team of horses drink. If that was the case, then they were keeping pace with him.

Linc planned on stopping at a small settlement called Sahuarita. There wasn't much there; it was nothing more than a trading post with a few nearby dwellings. At least he could get something to drink and give the horses a rest there.

He was about two miles from Sahuarita when he lost sight of the riders again. As he looked around to try and spot them, he saw another rider atop a ridge to his right. The lone rider was also riding in the same direction as Linc was headed.

"Three riders heading north," Linc said aloud. "And not riding the stagecoach road...strange; very strange indeed."

What Linc didn't know was that the three men were Whitey Howard, Joe Carson, and Pony Deal. Whitey was waiting for the right spot to waylay Linc. Whitey wanted Linc to know that he was being watched.

Whitey Howard's full name was Howard Haisley, but due to his near white blond hair had picked up the nickname of 'Whitey'. He had dropped the family name, not wanting to soil it with his outlaw deeds. Something Whitey took pride in relaying to those he knew.

Haisley had come to Arizona from the Spokane Falls area of Washington State. He'd gotten into some trouble there when he shot a deputy sheriff who tried to arrest him for disorderly conduct. The deputy died a few days after the shooting and a five hundred dollar reward was put on his head.

Whitey had headed for the gold fields of California, but didn't remain there for long. He crossed over the Sierra Nevada Mountain Range into Nevada and wound up in Virginia City. Another shooting there had forced him to Arizona where he'd hooked up with Ike Carter.

He was still carrying a grudge against Linc Sackett for the killing of one of his good friends, Brice Dalton. That same day Sackett had also killed one of Howard's acquaintances, a man by the name of Charlie Plimpton. Whitey's vendetta, however, was solely due to the killing of Dalton.

Whitey looked across the stagecoach road in the direction of Deal and Carson and waved when he got their attention. He kicked his horse into a gallop signaling Carson and Deal to do the same. They moved quickly ahead of Linc and the buckboard.

Sackett saw the three of them riding hard atop the ridges. He knew something was up, he just didn't know what. There wasn't much he could do to avoid whatever it was the three had planned. About all he could do was to be ready for whatever happened.

Linc slowed the team of horses to a walk. He didn't want to rush into trouble. He'd been around enough to know that sometimes quail or small birds could warn a person if something wrong was afoot. He'd just had that thought when he saw a covey of quail fly out of a draw up ahead. Something had scared them; Linc figured it was one of the riders; or it could have been all three.

This was getting a little too serious to Linc's way of thinking. He pulled the team to a halt and listened for a sound that might tell him something. He'd just about given up on that idea when he heard the snort of a horse. It came from the draw next to the road from where the quail had been spooked.

Linc picked up his rifle and checked to make sure there was a cartridge in the chamber. He laid the rifle across his lap and cocked the hammer back. If someone was laying a trap he wanted to be ready for it.

A slight movement of some brush near the road was all it took to send Linc diving out of the

*Five Faces West*

buckboard and landing behind a good sized rock. Just as he did a bullet ricocheted off the rock he had taken cover behind.

Linc couldn't see anyone but had a general idea where the shot had come from. He fired two shots in the direction of the brush near the road. Three more shots rang out; each coming from a different gun.

It was obvious that the three men he'd seen riding the ridges were the ones shooting at him; but who were they, Linc wondered? He'd made some enemies over the years so it could be anyone of a half dozen people.

Looking around the area, Linc saw that the draw he was lying near had good cover if he could make it down there. He'd have to make another rolling dive, but it would be worth it...he hoped.

Taking a deep breath and counting to three, he got to his feet in a crouching position while keeping well concealed behind the rock. When he said "3" he made his move. Shots rang out as he did a somersault over the bank of the gully. He landed on the gully floor hard and had the wind knocked out of him momentarily. He quickly recovered though and moved in the direction of the bushwhackers.

Linc got just a glimpse of two men half concealed in the brush; he dropped to one knee and wasted no time in firing as fast as he could in the direction of the men. One of the men let out a loud yelp as though he'd been winged.

Linc lay flat on his stomach to make himself as small a target as he possibly could. One more shot was fired at him, but didn't even come close. It was merely a shot to keep him at a distance. Just after the shot was fired, he heard the sound of hoof beats as the bushwhackers made a hasty getaway.

Running back up the bank of the draw, Linc saw the three men riding hard up a hill off to his left. He figured they'd had the fight taken out of them for the time being. He knew, however, that he'd have to be alert to the possibility of another attempt by the men.

With all the shooting the wagon team had run on up the road in the direction of Sahuarita. Linc started walking, but saw the buckboard about three hundred yards up ahead. The horses had managed to find some grass and had stopped to graze.

Linc walked up to the buckboard and climbed aboard. He took another good look around to make sure his attackers weren't returning and then snapped the harness reins and headed the horses on up the road.

The attempted ambush preyed on Linc's mind as he rode along. He hoped that Miss Shauna wouldn't be in any danger once he'd picked her up. One thing about her, though, she was a woman of Western spirit. She'd seen her share of danger and had made it through like the real woman she was.

He could take a liking to her, but it was common knowledge around the ranch that Buck had his sights set on her. It wasn't really clear what Miss Shauna thought of him, though. She seemed to like him, but didn't seem to be mad about him. At least that's the way Linc saw it.

What Linc didn't know was that Shauna had set her sights on him the very first day saw him. She hadn't let on to anyone about her feelings, but it was obvious to some that she seemed to do a lot more smiling when Linc showed up around the ranch house.

**Raymond D. Mason**

# Chapter 14

**The Southern Emigrant Trail
30 miles east of Carlsbad**

Brent had told Grant to take the reins of the wagon; he wanted to check the trail ahead and see what the terrain looked like. He kicked his saddle horse up and rode to the top of a hill. The traveling would be a little easier once they got over this hill; at least for what appeared to be three, maybe four miles.

Traveling in a wagon was slow going. Fortunately Julia and he didn't have a lot of furniture to haul with them, and Grant Holt and his wife were living on bare necessities when she died, so their wagon wasn't over loaded by any means.

The map that Brent had picked up indicated that there was a watering hole about forty miles from Santa Fe. There was no sign of it that Brent could see from where he was atop the hill.

He started to rein his horse around when he saw a small plume of dust off in the distance. He felt his pulse quicken when he remembered what he'd heard people in town talking about. They said there were some Mexican bandits had been attacking some of the homesteads and were robbing wagons moving West.

As he watched the dust cloud he breathed a sigh of relief when he saw the man riding behind the lead rider carrying a US Cavalry flag. It was a patrol. He reined his horse around and headed back towards their wagon.

"There's a cavalry patrol heading this way. Maybe they can tell us if there's been any Indian activity in the area. No one in town had heard of any; of course, they did warn us about the Mexican gang," Brent said.

"Do you think we'll be safe traveling by ourselves like this," Julia asked?

"I'm hoping the patrol can tell us if there've seen a wagon train up ahead. If not then we'll go on alone. We'll handle whatever comes our way, right Grant," Brent said with a half grin.

"Yes Julia, there's nothing to worry about," Grant said giving Brent a quick look.

The cavalry patrol topped the hill and rode on down to where they had stopped. The lieutenant in charge raised his hand for the troopers to halt.

"Hello folks," the lieutenant said with a polite salute, "Where are you headed...Arizona or California?"

"California, Lieutenant. Any trouble up ahead that you might have seen," Brent asked?

"We didn't see any, but we're on the trail of a Mexican gang who has been giving us some trouble. I must say, you are pretty brave traveling alone like this," the lieutenant said.

"We were with a wagon train, but they are taking the Old Spanish Trail to intersect with the California Trail and I've heard that road is might hard for wagons," Brent replied.

"You're right there," the lieutenant said with a serious look on his face. "How many wagons were in the wagon train?"

"Over thirty; like I said we left them when they turned north for Santa Fe," Brent said and looked at Julia. "My wife is expecting and I didn't want to take a chance on going that route if it was as rugged as I'd heard."

"You heard right. I can't figure out why any responsible wagon master would take his people on that trail. It's suicide," the lieutenant said shaking his head.

"The wagon master said he'd traveled the route and it wasn't as hard as people have said. But, you say it is, huh?"

"Yes, I should know; we've had skirmishes along that old trail as recent as six months ago. What was this wagon master's name," the lieutenant asked?

"The wagon master is Major John Harper Dupree and his scout is Jim Bowers. Have you heard of them," Brent asked?

The lieutenant slowly shook his head negatively, "No, the name doesn't ring a bell. But I'll tell you this. If he said he'd ridden that trail recently and it wasn't as difficult as people have said…he's lying."

Brent looked quickly at Julia and then at Grant. A thought crossed his mind and he quickly relayed it on to the lieutenant.

"Could it be that Major Dupree might be planning to rob the people in the wagon train?"

The lieutenant studied the question for a moment and then slowly nodded his head yes, "It could be. There have been incidents like that. The fact that he is taking them on that route indicates either complete incompetence or a possible robbery."

"I'd sure hate for those folks to be intended victims of the major's," Brent said.

"I wish we could help, but we're under strict orders to locate this Mexican gang and it looks like they're headed to Carlsbad. I'll let the Territorial Marshal know what you told me as soon as we get there, but that's about all I can do," the lieutenant said.

"Thanks, Lieutenant; I'm hoping I'm wrong about this," Brent stated.

"Well, we'd better get a move on. I hope you folks have a safe journey, and good luck in California."

The lieutenant tipped his hat and gave the order for the troopers to follow him. Brent, Julia, and Grant watched them ride away. Just as Grant started to turn his attention to the road ahead, something caught his eye. It was a wagon.

"Brent, look back there. There's a wagon moving this way," Grant said.

Brent shielded the sun from his eyes with his hand and after a few moments stated, "You're right, Grant. Now I wonder who that might be."

"Should we wait for them," Julia asked?

"Yeah, I think we should. If they're heading our way it makes it that much safer," Brent answered.

"Hey...you know what," Grant said as he continued to watch the wagon. "I think that wagon was with the wagon train. I remember it because of the canvas being a dark gray. It was the only one with a canvas like that in the train."

Brent took another hard look at the wagon and then nodded knowingly. He glanced at Julia and then said, "Grant's right. I know who that is."

"Who is it," Julia questioned?

"It's my old friend from Crystal City...Denver Dobbs."

"Are you sure, Brent? Wait, he did tell me that he would be taking another trail north once we reached Santa Fe. This must be that trail he was talking about," Julia said thoughtfully.

"Yeah, he did say that, didn't he," Brent said watching the approaching wagon.

When Dobbs finally reached them he reined up and smiled widely. It was quite obvious he was glad to have met up with another wagon with which to make the trek west.

"Well, what a pleasant surprise. I wasn't looking forward to making the remainder of the trip all by my lonesome," Dobbs said happily.

"I take it this is the route you told us you knew about," Brent replied.

"Yep, this is it. I've never traveled it by wagon, but I have ridden it by horseback before. It's got some rough spots, but it sure beats the route the major is taking those folks on," Dobbs said seriously.

"Yeah...that's just what that cavalry lieutenant was saying," Brent replied.

Brent looked around and spotted a grove of trees, "It's getting late in the day. I'd say this is as good a place as any to make camp. What do you say, Dobbs?"

"If you don't mind my opinion, Johnson, I'd say about two miles further up will be better. There's water and good cover," Dobbs said confidently.

"Two miles farther it is then," Brent said.

# Chapter 15

**El Paso, Texas**

**Black Jack Haggerty** and **Bonita Brand** arrived in town on the stagecoach and Jack quickly got a hotel room for them. Bonita had the most baggage, that being a good sized trunk and a carpetbag. Haggerty had his bedroll and saddle bags.

They went up to the room and Bonita told Jack she wanted to clean up from the dusty trip in the stagecoach. He agreed and said he was going to check on getting them a horse and carriage. He left while his pretty traveling companion proceeded to have a bath drawn for her.

Haggerty located a livery stable and asked the owner if he had any carriages for sale. The man said he didn't, but told him of a man in town who traded in such things. Haggerty went to see him and was able to work a deal out with the man.

By the time he got back to the hotel Bonita had finished her bath and was dressed in a shear negligee; something that was out of the ordinary for the women Haggerty was used to being with.

"My, oh my...what have we here," Haggerty said upon entering the room?

"A clean woman," Bonita replied.

"I love a clean woman," Haggerty said with a grin.

"Oh, is that right," Bonita said wryly?

"I should say so. Now let's get down to some serious 'getting to know one another'," Haggerty said as he gave his hat a sling towards a wall hook.

"Huh, uh...no way, Jack. Not until you've washed a couple of pounds of Texas dust off your body, along with anything else that might be there. I like my men clean," Bonita said firmly.

"Hey, I took a bath two weeks ago; well, it was sort of a bath. I had to ford a river and got soaked to the skin," Haggerty said seriously.

"I mean a real bath with soap. As you can see, the tub is still here just waiting for you."

Haggerty frowned and started to protest, but Bonita let the negligee fall open slightly, revealing just enough skin to widen his eyes. He instantly started undressing, shucking clothes left and right.

Haggerty climbed into the tub and closed his eyes at the refreshing feel of the still warm water. He laid his head back but opened his eyes quickly when Bonita put a cigar to his lips.

With wide eyes he asked, "Where'd you get this?"

"I had the Mexican woman who drew my bath for me get one from the front desk. I thought you might like one," Bonita said as she struck a match and lit the cigar.

Haggerty looked up at her and grinned as he took a long puff off the cigar.

After exhaling the smoke he said, "You know how to take care of a man, I must say."

"Honey, you ain't seen 'nothin' yet," Bonita grinned coyly.

She turned to walk away, but Haggerty grabbed her around the waist and pulled her into the tub with him. She let out a slight scream, but it was one of surprise mixed with delight. The two of them splashed around as Haggerty dropped the cigar to the floor next to the tub.

Once the splashing, laughing, and kissing stopped, Bonita climbed out of the tub. The sheer, soaking wet, negligee clung to her body making it all but transparent. Haggerty leered lustily.

"Now look what you've done, Jack. I'll have to take this wet thing off," Bonita cooed as she slowly and seductively untied the draw string and let the negligee drop to the floor.

## 30 miles north of Santa Angela, Texas

The three Comanche warriors chased Brian and AJ for over a mile before giving up and turning back towards the others. The brothers continued to ride hard wanting to put as much distance as possible between them, the Comanches, and the Texas Rangers.

After riding for at least five miles the boys stopped in a grove of trees miles from where the Texas Rangers had been jumped by the Comanche war party. They sat for a while looking back the way they had come to make sure they weren't being followed.

"I guess the rangers were forced to forget about us," AJ said.

"I feel bad that we couldn't stay and give them a hand, but we wouldn't have been much use to them with no guns and our hands cuffed like this," Brian said looking down at the handcuffs on his hands.

"I'm not all that sad we couldn't stay with 'em. Their hair may be hanging from a Comanche wikkiup about now. D'you think you can get these off of us," AJ asked?

"I don't know. I think so. Let's get down so I can take a better look at them."

They climbed down out of their saddles and Brian looked closely at the handcuffs.

"So what do you think, Brian...can you get 'em off," AJ asked impatiently?

"Hold your horses, AJ," Brian said as he inspected the cuffs. "Yeah, I don't see any problem."

"Do you want to use my pocket knife," AJ asked.

"No, I have something better than that if I can get it out of my pocket," Brian said.

Brian managed to get a horseshoe nail out of his shirt pocket and inserted it into the handcuff's key slot. He worked with the nail for a few seconds, listening as he slowly moved it from one side to the other.

"Do you always walk around with a horseshoe nail in your pocket like that," AJ asked curiously?

"Yeah, what's so unusual about that? I have two horseshoes in my saddlebags along with nails and a hammer and pliers," Brian replied.

"You really came prepared, didn't you little brother."

Just then the clasp on the cuff ring snapped open. Brian grinned as he cast a quick look at AJ. He was able to merely pull the other ring loose.

"Well, I got mine," Brian said as he dropped the handcuffs in his saddlebags and started to climb back in the saddle.

"Hey...what about me," AJ said with a concerned look on his face.

"Oh, I'm sorry, AJ. Here you go," Brian said and handed him the horseshoe nail. "Have at it."

"Wha...," AJ said with his mouth hanging open and a frown on his face?

When Brian saw AJ standing there with his mouth a gape he couldn't contain himself and broke into laughter.

"Oh, you want me to do it," Brian asked innocently?

"Uh...yeah," AJ replied.

Working with his hands free Brian soon had the cuffs off of AJ as well. The two mounted up and headed for San Angela.

Due to the route they had been forced to take during their escape, there was no way they could pick up the trail of Rawhide Deacon and Snake Eyes Bob. Now they would be forced to ride straight to San Felipe del Rio and try to locate the whereabouts of Deacon's brother's place. The first thing they would have to do, however, was pick up some guns somewhere.

It was close to midnight when AJ and Brian arrived in Santa Angela. The town had been named after the founder, Bartholomew DeWitt's wife, Angela. It would later be changed to San Angelo.

They got a room in the only hotel in town and went right to sleep. Around one o'clock in the morning, however, they were awakened by a commotion in the street. Brian rushed to the window and looked out.

There were over a dozen men on horseback gathered down the street in front of the Outpost Saloon. Brian recognized one of the men as one of the Texas Rangers who was to escort them to ranger's headquarters; the man named Ed; the one who had high-tailed it away from the battle.

"AJ, look at this," Brian said, giving AJ a wave.

"What is it? Man, I'm sleepy," AJ complained, but got up and moved to the window.

Looking out at the riders, AJ quickly spotted the Texas Ranger who was addressing the other riders.

"Hey, that's the ranger that rode away from the fight. What's he doing heading up a posse to go after the Comanches?"

AJ raised the window in their room and they could hear the ranger named Ed saying, "The Comanche war party that jumped us was small; maybe eight, nine warriors. They were equipped with repeating rifles though and took us by surprise; they probably obtained the rifles from trade with the Comancheros. They killed all the rangers but me and two prisoners who escaped during the attack.

"Those red sticks chased me for over two hours. I tell you I only escaped by a miracle. I stayed until I was the last man standing before high-tailing it out of that box canyon."

"I say we go after them since the cavalry has most of their men up north searching for those very same Comanches and the rest of the troops are down with influenza. If we don't move now none of you are going to be safe," the ranger said.

"What are we waiting for," someone in the crowd yelled out.

"Yeah, let's go," another man agreed.

"I'll take you to where we were attacked and we'll pick up their trail there with no trouble once it gets light," the ranger called out, and then said, "Let's ride."

AJ turned away from the window and looked at Brian. The look on his face expressed exactly what Brian was thinking, as well.

"Now what do you make of that," AJ asked curiously. "This guy runs away from the fight and now he's gonna lead a posse to do battle? I don't believe it."

"Maybe he had a guilty conscience and this is his way of soothing it," Brian suggested.

"Yeah, but I've got news for him...it won't work. If they catch up to the Comanche war party, which is highly doubtful, he ain't going to suddenly find his back bone. He'll run when push comes to shove," AJ said thoughtfully.

"Well, we can't worry about it now; let's get some shuteye," Brian said and went back to bed.

# Chapter 16

Brian and AJ picked up a couple of six shooters and two Henry repeating rifles the next morning before hitting the trail for San Felipe del Rio. A small café on the outskirts of town was open and they grabbed a couple of burritos and ate them as they rode.

It was over one hundred and fifty dangerous miles from Santa Angela to San Felipe del Rio due to the gangs from both sides of the border that roamed these parts. They encountered no trouble along the way fortunately.

The Sackett brothers covered over forty miles a day and on the fourth day arrived in San Felipe del Rio around six o'clock in the evening. The first thing they did was to find a decent hotel and then board their horses at the nearest livery stable. Then they treated themselves to a large meal in the hotel restaurant and sat back to enjoy a fine cigar.

Brian looked at AJ and said, "In the morning we'll see the sheriff and find out if he can help us locate Rawhide Deacon's brother's place."

"We don't even know Deacon's last name. Unless Deacon is known around here by that moniker we may have trouble finding his brother," AJ replied.

"I've been doing a lot of thinking, AJ and I recall hearing someone at the ranch say they thought his brother had a business in town here. I don't remember what business it was that he had, but even if he's sold it by now, someone will remember him," Brian said.

"You mean to tell me you've known this all the time and you're just now telling me about it? But I say again, we don't know what Deacon's real name is."

"I haven't known it all this time; I just remembered it, that's all," Brian said with a wry grin.

"Well, at least that narrows our odds down a little bit. But like I said, we still don't know his last name," AJ replied.

"I'll bet you five dollars that Rawhide Deacon has a wanted poster on him. You can't have a temper like he does and not have some paper on you for something," Brian said and blew a plume of grey blue smoke into the air.

"Excuse me sir, but do you have to blow that cigar smoke in our direction," a woman's voice said to Brian's right.

Brian looked quickly up into the face of a beautiful woman. He sat upright and stared at the woman, but didn't answer her right away.

AJ looked from the woman to Brian and said, "Well, aren't you going to say anything, little brother?"

"Oh, uh, no...I mean yes," Brian fumbled with his words before finally saying, "I'm sorry, Ma'am I'll watch where I smoke the blow...I mean, blow the smoke from now on. In fact I won't blow it at all...uh, I mean, I'll put this thing out."

The woman smiled demurely and said, "You don't have to put it out, just don't blow it towards our table. My little girl has an asthmatic condition and gets choked up by the smoke."

"Oh, I'm sorry to hear that. I'll definitely watch my smoke...and his, my brother's smoke as well," Brian gushed.

"Thank you, I truly appreciate it," the woman said and turned to go back to her table.

"You are one silver tongued devil; did you know that, little brother?"

"What...what did I say," Brian asked with a frown?

"I tell you, you would sweep any woman right off their feet," AJ chuckled.

"And I suppose you would do a lot better, huh?"

"I wouldn't let my tongue get over my eye teeth so I couldn't see what I was saying," AJ laughed.

"Oh, yeah...well...what?"

"There you go again. You are one great orator, little brother."

"Hey, watch that name calling," Brian said.

Brian continued to cast quick glances at the woman and her daughter. The woman looked familiar to him, but he couldn't remember where he had seen her. AJ noticed and asked about it.

"What's eatin' at you?"

"That woman...she sure looks familiar," Brian said.

"She probably told you to put your cigar out in another restaurant somewhere."

"No, no...it wasn't anything like that," Brian said with a frown.

The woman, also, kept casting glances towards Brian. She thought he looked familiar also, but like Brian, couldn't remember where they'd met. When their eyes met, Brian smiled warmly and she returned it.

Suddenly Brian's face lit up as he recalled where the two had met. It was when he was on his way home from Laredo over a year before. She worked in the telegraph office he'd stopped at to deliver a letter from her husband who had been killed by a Comanche war party. He couldn't remember her name, though.

As Brian set their trying to remember her name, AJ pulled out his pocket watch and checked it. He held it up to his ear and then started to wind the stem. It was his comment that jogged Brian's memory in regards to the woman's name.

"I forget that I'm carrying this thing and I'm always forgetting to wind it," AJ stated.

"That's it," Brian exclaimed as he snapped his finger. "Wind it...I mean Wanda; Wanda Thalheimer and her little girl Abby."

"What the devil are you talking about, Brian?"

"The woman who asked me not to blow smoke in their direction; her name is Wanda Thalheimer and the little girl is named Abby. I delivered a letter to her from her husband who had been killed

111

by Comanches," Brian said and looked back towards the pretty woman.

"Well, well; it's a small world, isn't it? Go over and tell her. I want to see how you handle this," AJ grinned.

"I'll do just that," Brian said and stood up.

Brian walked over to where the woman sat and smiled, "Excuse me Mrs. Thalheimer, I knew I'd seen you before and I just remembered where it was. I delivered a letter to you from your husband awhile back."

"Oh, yes, I remember you. To be honest I thought we'd met, but couldn't remember where or when it was," Wanda said warmly. "I'm afraid I don't remember much about that day after I received the letter. What is your name?"

"Brian Sackett and that's my brother AJ over there. I'm sure glad I remembered where it was we'd met. That would have driven me crazy until I finally remembered."

"So am I. I certainly wouldn't want you going crazy on my account," Wanda said with a slight chuckle.

"No Ma'am, me neither," Brian said with a big grin. "So what brings you to San Felipe del Rio?"

"I'm here to see an old friend. She owns a dress shop here in town and asked me to come down and visit for awhile. She just lost her husband a few months back," Wanda said.

"Has she lived here long?"

"Yes, about six years now."

"My brother and I sure would like to speak with her. We're here looking for a man who had a business here, but we don't know his name."

"Oh, what kind of business did he have?"

Brian blushed slightly, "Well, we think it might have been a saloon."

Wanda smiled, "You don't have a lot to go on, do you?"

"No, we sure don't Mrs. Thalheimer."

Just then Mrs. Thalheimer's friend entered the dining area. She was about the same age as Wanda and Brian. She made her way over to Wanda's table and when she arrived gave Brian a questioning look before sitting down.

"Joyce, this is Mr. Brian Sackett," Wanda said, "Remember me telling you about the letter that was delivered to me about my husband's death. Well, Mr. Sackett is the man who delivered it. We were just recalling our meeting."

"Oh, hello, I'm Joyce Ross. Wanda and I have been friends forever," Joyce smiled.

"Yes, that's what she said," Brian replied.

"Mr. Sackett and his brother, there, are looking for a man whose last name they do not know, who may or may not have owned a saloon here in town, and was wondering if you knew the man," Wanda said laughingly.

"I know it sounds crazy, but there's a long story goes with it," Brian said with a grin.

"Well, why don't you have your brother join us and you can explain it all," Joyce said giving AJ a quick glance.

"If you don't mind, we'd love to do just that," Brian said enthusiastically.

Brian motioned to AJ to join them. The men took a seat and began to tell the ladies the story behind their being there. The evening went along very well, although Joyce was unable to give them any information about Rawhide Deacon's brother.

# Chapter 17

### Somewhere along The Trail to Las Cruces

**Brent** looked back at Dobb's wagon and shook his head, "I don't know why I don't trust that guy. He hasn't really done anything to make me feel this way, but I do. Has he said anything to you that I should know about," Brent asked Julia?

"No, not a word, Brent; if he knows you from Crystal City he sure isn't letting on about it," Julia answered.

"I can't say I'm not glad that he's joined up with us, but I just wish I wasn't so suspicious. I think tonight I'll just come right out and ask him if he knows anything about my trouble in Crystal City," Brent stated.

"Do you think that would be a wise thing to do, Brent? He might think there's a reward on your head and turn you in for it," Julia said with concern.

"I'll have to take my chances. I think it's better to get this out in the open so I don't have to be worrying about it anymore," Brent stated.

"Well, do what you think is the right thing to do. I wouldn't, but that's just me," Julia said.

Grant Holt had ridden on ahead to see if he could spot a good place to camp and was about two miles from the wagons. He topped a hill and quickly reined his horse to a halt. About a half mile away he saw three wagons that had been burned; and recently.

Grant quickly looked around the area to see if he was being watched. He couldn't see anyone, but knew the ones who had done this couldn't be too far away; the wagons were still smoldering.

Grant turned his horse around and kicked it into a full run back in the direction of Brent and Dobbs wagons. He continued to scan the surrounding terrain for any sign of trouble.

When Brent saw Grant approaching at full gallop he knew something was wrong. When Grant rode up to the wagon he told Brent what he'd seen.

"And the wagons were still smoking," Brent questioned?

"Yeah, not much, mind you; but they were still smoking."

"Did you see any sign of Indians...arrows...unshod pony tracks...anything like that," Brent asked?

"To be honest, Brent, all I wanted to do was get back here and let you know what I'd seen," Grant said truthfully.

"Yeah, good; you sure don't want to run the risk of getting caught out there alone. Okay, we'll keep our eyes peeled for any sign of trouble. Go back and tell Dobbs what you saw," Brent said.

Grant rode back to let Dobbs know what he'd seen and Julia asked Brent what he thought.

"Do you think it might be Indians?"

"I don't know. I'm more concerned about outlaw gangs along this route than I am about Indians; so many of the Indian tribes are on reservations now. Of course, there's always the threat of a band of renegades that are fed up with the poor living conditions who leave the reservations and start hitting small ranches and homesteads," Brent said.

"And small wagon trains," Julia asked?

"And small wagon trains," Brent stated.

They moved on until they came to the spot where the burned wagons were located. Brent got down from the wagon and checked the area for hoof prints as he walked towards the back wagon. He found plenty.

"These tracks weren't made by Indian ponies. These tracks all have horseshoes; this was done by bandits," Brent stated as he walked up to the wagon and looked inside.

Brent quickly looked away from the grisly scene in the wagon, but once the shock had worn off, returned to look upon the burned bodies inside.

"Stay away from the wagons, Julia," Brent warned.

Dobbs cast a quick look at Brent and then moved to where he could see into the bed of the wagon. He, too, looked away quickly. Grant didn't bother to look, figuring correctly that it was something he'd rather not see.

"I'm going to check the other wagons," Brent said as he walked away from the first one.

There was no one in the second or third wagon which caused Brent to look around the surrounding area. A slight movement from some brush caught Brent's eye. More movement in the area caused him to pull his pistol.

Dobbs was watching Brent and when he saw him draw his gun, did the same. The two of them moved cautiously towards the small cluster of brush.

"Come out of there," Brent called out.

Nothing happened at first, but then a boy of about ten years of age stood up and held his hands in the air. The young boy stepped out into the open and looked back behind him.

"Don't shoot, Mister. We don't have any guns," the boy said.

"Well, I'll be...," Brent said and stuck his gun back in its holster; Dobbs did the same.

"Are you by yourself," Brent asked as he moved slowly towards the boy?

"No, sir; I have a little sister," the boy said.

"We're not going to hurt you. We're here to help you. Have your sister come out," Brent said evenly.

The boy looked from Brent to Dobbs and then back towards the brush, "Come on out, Annie; it's okay," he said.

A small girl of about five years of age slowly walked out to where her brother was standing.

They both looked scared as they moved slowly in Brent and Dobbs direction.

"We're not going to hurt you," Brent said again with a slight smile.

"What happened here," Brent asked?

The boy slowly put his hands down, but the little girl didn't. When the boy noticed he gently pushed his sister's hands down to her side.

"Bandits came and attacked us. They shot our folks and took what they wanted; then they burned the wagons," the boy said slowly.

"How'd you manage to get away," Brent asked as the kids walked up to him and Dobbs?

"I had gone with her to keep an eye on her while she went...potty. While we were down there behind that brush the men came riding up shooting and yelling. They didn't see us. At first I wanted to help the folks, but then I thought of Annie and just stayed where we were."

Brent looked at the two kids and his heart ached at what they'd seen, as well as what they would face. He put his hand on the boy's shoulder, feeling the little fella stiffen slightly.

"You'll go with us. This man is named Dobbs and I'm Brent. That young man there is Grant. And the pretty lady walking this way is my wife, Julia," Brent said evenly.

Julia hurried to where they were and put her arms around the little girl. Annie stiffened against the hug.

"She's scared to death, Brent," Julia said.

"Take care of them, would you, honey. Move our wagon on down the trail and Dobbs and I will take care of the...remains," Brent said.

119

Julia escorted the two kids to the wagon and loaded them aboard. She drove the team on down the trail a ways so they wouldn't see what the men had to do.

"What're your names," Julia asked?

The boy, looking downcast said slowly, "My name is Hank Thurston and this is my sister Annie."

Julia looked tenderly at the two children, knowing how they must feel at that moment. She was struck by how the boy didn't seem to be nearly as upset as he might have been over the loss of his parents.

Once Brent and Dobbs had finished burying the remains of the people who had been shot and then their bodies loaded into one of the wagons and burned they held a simple burial ceremony.

Julia asked Brent if he would say words over the graves, and thinking of the kids, got no real resistance from him. He kept it simple; very simple.

"Lord, these folks are in Your hands now. I'm sure You'll know what to do with them. Amen," Brent said, holding his hat in his hands with his head bowed low.

Once that was taken care of they loaded up and moved on. They found a good place to make camp for the night about three miles from the spot where the attack on the other wagons had occurred.

Julia had noticed the terrible condition of the little girl's dress and took one of her blouses and adjusted it to fit Annie. When she took the little girl's dress off of her, she noticed the red marks across Annie's back.

"Brent, come here a second, would you," Julia said in an even tone of voice so as not to frighten Annie.

Brent moved over to where Julia was and she nodded towards Annie's back. Brent frowned deeply as he looked at the unmistakable sign of a beating. He cast a quick look at Julia and nodded his acknowledgement. Brent went back to where Hank was sitting at the fire with Dobbs and put his hand on the boy's shoulder.

"Do you have a night shirt, Hank," Brent asked?

"I did have, but it was in the wagon and burned up with the rest of our stuff," Hank said.

"Well, you can wear one of my shirts, how's that. It'll be a little big on you, but it should do the job," Brent said with a smile.

"Hank can bed down in my wagon with me and Grant since you and Julia will have the little girl with you," Dobbs said.

"Thanks, Dobbs. Let me get that shirt for you, Hank. Come with me," Brent said.

Hank went with Brent to the wagon and Brent grabbed one of his three shirts and held it up to see how it would fit the boy. It would be much too big, but for a nightshirt it would serve the purpose just fine.

"Let me see how this is going to fit you," Brent said. "Get your shirt off."

Hank unbuttoned his shirt and laid it aside. Brent moved around so he could get a look at the boy's back and grimaced slightly when he saw the four long scars across Hank's back.

"How'd you get these scars on your back, Hank," Brent said matter-of-factly, "Fall over a barbed wire fence?"

Hank didn't say anything for a moment, but finally answered, "I got them from Mr. Gorton."

"Who's Mr. Gorton," Brent asked?

"Mr. Gorton and his wife took Annie and me in when our ma and pa were killed by Kiowas in Texas," Hank said.

"Oh, so the ones killed weren't your ma and pa then, but the Gorton's; is that right?"

"Yeah; I didn't mind the whippings I got so much, but when they started whipping Annie I got really mad at them. Once we got to California I was going to take Annie and run away," Hank said firmly.

Brent didn't say anything for a moment and then stated, "You don't have to worry about anyone whipping you now. They'll have me to deal with me if they try."

Hank looked at Brent with wide eyes and a grin slowly crawled across his face.

"Do you mean that?"

"I surely do. Julia will take good care of Annie. If you don't have any kinfolk anywhere you can live with us. How's that," Brent asked?

Hank's grin widened even more, "I think that's a good thing."

# Chapter 18

**Tucson, Arizona**

**Linc Sackett** picked up Miss Shauna at the stage depot in Tucson and suggested they get something to eat before heading back to the ranch. She was more than willing.

The two of them went to eat at the nicest place in Tucson and took a seat by the window. They ordered their meal and then made polite small talk for awhile before Linc finally told Shauna about the ambush. He hadn't planned on it, but thought it might be better just in case the men tried again.

"My lord, Linc; who would do such a thing," Shauna asked?

"I can think of several who might want to get back at me for certain things. I wasn't ever in a position to get a good look at any of the three's faces, so they're a mystery to me," Linc stated.

"What about the ones who were caught stealing our cattle; do you think it might have been them," Shauna asked?

"It wasn't two of them, I can tell you that. There was one man who got away that could possibly be involved. If they talk about it, though, it will eventually get back to me," Linc said and looked out the window.

The street was fairly crowded but the three men on horseback that were just riding past the eatery caught Linc's eye. One of the horses; a black and white paint; looked familiar to him. One of the men who had been involved in the ambush was riding a black and white paint.

"Would you excuse me just a minute, Miss Shauna? I have to talk to a man about a horse," Linc said as he got up and dropped his napkin on the chair.

"Our food will be coming shortly, Linc. Will you be long?"

"No, I shouldn't be. It won't get cold, I can assure you of that," Linc said with a smile.

He walked out to the front and looked down the street in the direction the men were heading. They were just tying up in front of a saloon. Linc started walking towards them.

Whitey Howard stepped up on the boardwalk and looked around before entering the saloon. He started for the batwing doors, but did a double take when he saw the tall man striding towards them.

Whitey turned to his two cohorts and said, "Guess who's in town and headed our way?"

The two men turned to look in the direction that Whitey was looking. When they saw Linc, Joe Carson said, "It's Sackett."

Pony Deal looked at Linc, but then looked across the street in the direction of two other men.

"I also see another man; Henry Garfias, the Phoenix marshal. What's he doing down here in Tucson," Deal questioned?

"Garfias was asking around about you, Pony. You'd better make yourself scarce. I don't think you want to tangle with him. You and Whitey take off and leave Sackett to me," Carson stated.

"Come on, Pony; Joe we'll meet you at the saloon on the outskirts of town," Whitey said quickly as he untied his bridle reins and started climbing back into the saddle.

Pony hurriedly followed Whitey's lead and the two of them rode off leaving Joe Carson there to face Linc Sackett. Carson figured on making it appear that Linc drew first and he was just too fast for him.

Carson started walking towards Linc in a gunman's walk. His eyes darted from Linc to Henry Garfias and back to Linc. Pony Deal had taught Carson how to feint with one shoulder while going for his gun with the opposite arm. It makes it look like the other man is drawing first, when he isn't.

Linc had noticed that the man riding the paint horse was the man with very light blond hair; Whitey Howard. He also noticed that this man had been in the company of the other two men and now was heading his way.

When Carson was about twelve feet from Linc he stopped and feinted with his left shoulder as he went for his gun with his right hand. His move caught the eye of not only Linc, but Henry Garfias, as well. Garfias thought the man was going for his gun against him and drew his pistol just as Linc drew his.

The two gunshots sounded as one with both bullets hitting Carson at the same time. Carson flew backwards a good four feet and landed on his back; staring straight up towards a heaven he would never see.

Garfias turned quickly and aimed his gun at Linc, who also spun towards the marshal. The two men then turned and looked at the dead man lying in Tucson's main street. Garfias and the man he had been talking to started walking towards Carson's body as did Linc.

"Was he gunning for you...or me," Garfias asked?

"I think it was me," Linc answered.

"Do you know him?"

"No, I never laid eyes on him. He was with two other men, though, and I think they are the same three who tried to ambush me when I was on my way here," Linc said.

"Why would they do that," Garfias asked?

"I have no idea," Linc replied.

Just then Miss Shauna came running from the restaurant, but quickly slowed when she saw Carson's body. She looked at Linc and then walked up to him very slowly.

"Are you all right, Linc," she asked, peeking around him and taking one more quick look at the body.

"Yeah, I am. I can't say the same thing about this man, though," Linc said as Garfias walked over and began going through Carson's pockets.

"I was scared to death thinking you might have been hurt...or killed," Shauna said looking into Linc's eyes.

Linc grinned slightly, "Really? You really were concerned about me?"

Shauna looked a little surprised at his response, "Well, yes...of course. To be honest I would have been heart broken if anything happened to you."

Linc smiled at Shauna but wasn't sure what he should say. He looked at Garfias who had fished out a letter from Carson's pocket and was reading it.

"Did you find something on the guy's identity," Linc asked not knowing what else to say.

"Yeah, it looks like his name is Joe Carson; does that mean anything to you?"

"No, not a thing...who is the letter from," Linc asked.

"It's from a man by the name of Ike Carter; does that name mean anything to you?"

"That name does. He's a rancher out our way who deals in stolen cattle more than anything," Linc replied.

"Is that right? Perhaps I'd better do a little checking on that man," Garfias stated.

"Are you a lawman," Linc asked?

Garfias pulled back his vest and showed Linc his badge. My name is Henry Garfias; and you are?"

"Sackett, Linc Sackett."

"Well, I'd better get rid of this mess. You can go if you want to, Sackett," Garfias said. "You obviously shot in self defense...as did I."

"Thanks, Marshal; come on Miss Shauna," Linc said as he took Shauna's arm and started back towards the restaurant.

"You mean you can still eat after what just happened," Shauna asked?

"I can…he can't," Linc said looking back in the direction of Carson.

Shauna looked at Linc with unbelieving eyes. What kind of a man was he, anyway? He could actually eat lunch after nearly being killed and shooting a man dead? Either he was a cold blooded man or one who didn't let things like that bother him. She had to know which one it was due to the attraction she felt for him.

"Linc, doesn't it bother you to take a man's life?"

"Yes, it does. But, I'm convinced now that this Carson fella and the two he was with were the ones who tried to kill me on the road here today. Now, I'd much rather it hadn't happened, but it did and I can't change that.

"This was a case of kill or be killed. Carson lost. I won. I'm hungry…so let's eat," Linc said evenly.

"That's so, so…," Shauna started to say, but was cut off by Linc.

"Heartless; is that the word you're looking for?"

"Yes, I guess it is. It's just so unfeeling; so uncaring."

"I care greatly about taking a man's life; much more than that man cared about taking my life, obviously. I never met this Carson fella; so as far as I know, I never did anything to hurt him or make him mad, but he was going to kill me. I'm not going to lose sleep over something like that. Now if I'm wrong…I'm sorry, but that's the way it is," Linc explained.

Shauna thought about what Linc had said, but needed time to digest it. She was well aware of the fact that the West was a violent land and people sometimes had to take desperate measures just to survive. Still, however, his coolness bothered her.

**Raymond D. Mason**

# Chapter 19

**Somewhere in the Guadalupe Mountains**

**Denver Dobbs** rode along with the two Thurston children riding in his wagon with him. Hank sat on the bench seat next to Dobbs while little Annie rode in the back. They had managed to salvage a rag doll of the little girl's from one of the wagons the bandits had burned.

Hank was a quiet boy, holding a lot of his feelings inside. That suited Dobbs well, since he wasn't a big talker himself. The two rode in silence, each lost in thoughts only known to them. Annie hummed as she played mommy to the doll.

Looking around the inside of the wagon for something to use as blanket to cover up her rag doll with, Annie found a folded up paper stuck between the wooden wagon bed and the canvas covering.

Annie unfolded the paper and looked at it, but folded it back up and stuck it in her apron pocket. She soon forgot she even had the paper as she played make believe with the rag doll.

Brent and Julia were busy discussing their options with the children. They could turn them over to authorities and let them deal with the children; or, they could keep them with them, making sure they had a good home life. Julia was all for keeping them.

"I hate the thought of them going to another family that would beat them like the last ones did," Julia said.

"Julia, you have the Holt baby, plus you're carrying our baby, and now you want to take on two kids we know nothing about? I think it would be too much for you," Brent argued.

"Brent, my mother had six kids of her own and we took in two more whose folks were killed in a tornado. It wasn't easy, but we made it just fine. I think we should just go ahead and raise them like they are ours.

"Just look at little Annie tonight when we make camp. She adores you and is looking at me like I'm her mama. Hank is so mature for his age; I know he would be able to give you a hand with all the chores you're going to have," Julia said, making her point like a Philadelphia lawyer.

"Okay, okay...you know I can't refuse anything you want, Julia. It's settled...they're ours," Brent said getting a big hug from Julia.

That night after supper and they were all seated around the campfire, Annie got up and went to Dobbs wagon and grabbed her rag doll. When she came back she stuck her hand in her apron pocket and found the folded up paper. She took it out and opened it up to use it as her 'make believe' blanket.

No one paid much attention to the paper at first, but when Dobbs saw what Annie had he became very upset.

"Hey, give me that," Dobbs said as he tried to grab the paper from Annie, but missed.

"What is it, Dobbs," Brent wanted to know?

"It's nothing, just that I have some valuable papers in my wagon and I don't want this kid messing around with them," Dobbs groused.

"I'm sorry, Mr. Dobbs," Hank said and took the paper away from Annie. "She won't do it again."

"Let's see what it is, Hank," Brent asked and held his hand out.

Dobbs became upset at Brent and snatched the paper away from Hank before he could hand it to Brent.

"I don't like people snooping into my business," Dobbs said angrily, "and that goes for you too."

"Hey, hold on there, Dobbs. What's so important with that paper that you don't want anyone even looking at it," Brent said harshly.

"Like I said, it's no one's business but mine."

Brent glared at Dobbs for a few seconds and then said, "If you're traveling with someone and living in as close quarters as we are, I don't think there should be any secrets kept that might affect the others. I just want to know if that paper affects us in any way."

Dobbs and Brent glared hard at one another for a moment and then Dobbs stated, "Oh, like being on the run from the law, for instance."

Brent stiffened, "What do you mean by that? Are you on the run from the law?"

Dobbs shook his head negatively, "No, but you are," he said as he began to unfold the paper.

Holding it up so Brent and the others could see it, Dobbs said, "Looks like you have a little secret you've been keeping from folks, Sackett."

The paper was a wanted poster that Dobbs had picked up in Carlsbad. It read, 'Brent Sackett, Wanted for Murder and Robbery.' There was a $1,500 reward out for his capture, dead or alive.

"What are you planning to do, Dobbs, claim that reward," Brent asked evenly?

"No...I'm just going to California. I picked this up for insurance just in case you were against me going along with you."

"For some reason I find that hard to believe. If that was the case why didn't you just show me when you caught up to us?"

"What? And run the risk of you plugging me? I'm not a total fool. No, I just wanted to have something I could use as a bargaining chip. Besides, who am I going to run into out here that could honor this reward? Now that you know I have it, what are you going to do about it?"

Brent didn't answer right away as he thought of his options. He looked at Julia holding the baby, and then at Grant; then he looked at the two Thurston children and reassessed the situation.

Finally he said, "Nothing, Dobbs; not now anyway. I've got a responsibility to this woman and these kids. If, however, you decide to turn me in..., well, let's just say we'll cross that bridge when we come to it."

Dobbs looked from Brent to Julia and then back at Brent. He wasn't so sure now he had done the right thing in telling Brent what he knew about him. If it hadn't been for that little kid, he thought to himself.

Dobbs got up and went to his wagon. Brent and Julia sat quietly watching him and once he was out of ear shot, Julia spoke.

"What do you think he will do, Brent, turn you in for the reward?"

"I don't know. He'll wait until we get to California, though. He's a gambler and he's patient. One thing is sure; he planned on doing something about that wanted poster or he wouldn't have brought it with him. He may have been planning on making me his 'California stake'; in fact, he may still be planning on doing just that," Brent said thoughtfully.

"Why can't people just leave us alone," Julia said quietly.

"What was it I read in the Bible? Oh yeah, 'Be sure your sins will find you out'; well, it looks like that's true," Brent said.

Julia cocked her head to one side, "I didn't know you have read the Bible?"

Brent grinned slightly, "I picked yours up the other day and was reading while I drove the wagon. I sure wish we had that Sampson guy along with us."

Julia laughed lightly, but soon took on a more serious look.

"I wish I knew what Mr. Dobbs was going to do," she said thoughtfully.

Grant had been sitting with the kids and hadn't said a word. He got up and walked over to where

Brent and Julia were sitting and put his hand on Brent's shoulder.

"I don't know what that poster is all about, Brent. I only know that you and Julia came to help Grace when she was in trouble. You didn't know us at all and yet you were willing to try and help her.

"What you may or may not have done before that makes no difference to me. I'll stand by you as the friend I see you as. I just want you to know that," Grant said.

Brent grinned and glanced quickly at Julia, "Thanks for that, Grant. I did some things in the past that I'm sorry for now, but I can't change things back. All I can do now is to try and do the best I can from this point on."

Julia looked at Hank and Annie who were taking this all in. She smiled at them and said in a soft, kind voice, "There's nothing for you kids to worry about. Everything is fine. You'll see."

Brent listened to Julia's words and thought, 'I hope so'. If he had to get rid of Dobbs this would be the place to do it. No one would find his body out here; not for a long time; maybe never. But, he was trying to do the right thing now; he'd just told Grant so.

All Brent could do now was wait and see what Dobbs was up to. He looked up into the night sky that held a heaven full of stars and said, "If You're there...I need Your help."

# Chapter 20

### San Felipe del Rio, Texas

The morning after arriving in town **Brian** and **AJ** went to the sheriff's office. Once again they were faced with the problem of not knowing Rawhide Deacon's brother's name. They hit pay dirt, however, when they mentioned the name Rawhide Deacon. The sheriff did have a wanted poster on him.

"Yeah, I know this Deacon fella's brother. If you want to talk to him, though, you'll have to talk real loud," the sheriff said.

"Why...is he hard of hearing," AJ asked?

"No, he's dead. He got shot three days ago while dealing off the bottom of the deck. He owned a small spread about three miles from here, but I think the only thing he grew on it was 'tired'. He spent more time playing cards than he did working his land," the sheriff said.

"We have reason to believe that Deacon and another fella by the name of Snake Eyes Bob are headed this way and it's our guess they'll head for

Deacon's brother's place. Would you give us directions out to where it is," Brian asked?

"Sure I will. I don't want any trouble here in town, though. I don't like a lot of shootin' between factions if you know what I mean," the sheriff stated seriously.

"We're only here to take them back to stand trial for shooting our pa. If they put up a fight, though, we'll have to defend ourselves," AJ stated firmly.

"That's okay; just try and keep it out of the city limits. Then you'll be in a jurisdiction other than mine."

The brothers looked at one another and then back at the sheriff, "We give you our word."

"Here, I'll draw you a map of how to find Joe Dean's place. That's the brother's name," the sheriff said as he grabbed a wanted poster and scribbled a map on the back of it.

Brian and AJ rode up a draw that kept them out of sight of anyone who might be inside Joe Dean's small house. When they got to where they could see the back of the place, they spotted two horses in the corral.

"Doesn't that sorrel belong to Snake Eyes Bob," AJ asked?

"Yeah, and I recognize the bay as the one Deacon owned. They're in there all right."

"How do you want to work this," AJ asked?

"Let's draw them out of the house so we don't have to smoke 'em out. Let me get around to the back and let their horses out of the corral. You work your way over to that wagon near the corral and wait for 'em to come out. I'll be on the opposite side of the house and hopefully we can get the drop on 'em," Brian suggested.

"Okay; when I see the horses come by the house, I'll know you're in position," AJ said.

The two worked in opposite directions and took their places. Brian quietly opened the corral gate and got behind the horses and spooked them enough for them to run out of the corral and by the front of the house.

Since Deacon and Bob had the front door open, they could hear the sound of the hoof beats on the hard ground. Both men rushed out of the house in pursuit of the horses.

"Hold it right there, men," Brian yelled out.

Deacon and Bob whirled around and looked at Brian and as they did drew their guns.

"Don't do it," AJ yelled, causing them to whirl around and look in his direction. "Drop your guns."

Seeing they were caught in crossfire, Deacon and Bob dropped their guns and raised their hands. It looked as if they were going to give up peaceably. AJ and Brian moved out from behind their cover and started walking towards the two men.

They were about ten feet from where Deacon and Bob were standing when a voice called out to them from behind them.

"Hold it right there, boys," a man's voice said. "I've got a Winchester pointed at the middle of your back right now. Now...you boys drop your guns."

AJ and Brian froze. They hadn't seen anyone else around the cabin; where'd this guy come from and who was he?  They did as they were told and dropped their guns.

"Step back now and turn around very, very slow," the man ordered.

Deacon and Bob began laughing as they quickly picked up their guns.  Brian and AJ turned around and looked at the man holding the rifle.  It was the sheriff of San Felipe del Rio.

"Well, look who's here, Brian; it's the sheriff," AJ said with a deep frown.

"I see that, AJ.  I guess we went to the right man when we went to see the sheriff.  Naturally he would know Deacon's brother.  Birds of a feather, you know," Brian answered.

The sheriff, Deacon, and Bob began to laugh.  What they saw so funny escaped the Sackett's until they learned the joke was on them.

"What's so unusual about a man knowing his own brother," the sheriff said causing Deacon and Bob to laugh even harder.

"You went to the one person in town you should have avoided at all costs," Deacon continued to laugh.

"I thought your brother owned a business in town," Brian said.

"He does; he owns three businesses.  Two of them are saloons and the third is a sporting house," Deacon said gradually getting himself under control.

"So, what are you going to do with us," AJ asked?

"You're going to meet with a little accident.  We've been having trouble with bandits robbing and killing people on this side of the border.  We're going to hear some shooting and arrive too late to help you boys," the sheriff said.

"We have people here in town that will be asking questions, Sheriff," Brian said hoping to put some doubt in the sheriff's mind.

"I don't think so. Even if you do, I'll just play dumb," the sheriff said.

"That certainly won't be hard for you," AJ cracked.

"Let's not get personal now," the sheriff said and then added, "Come on, we're going for a little ride. Not far, mind you, just a mile or so away from my place here."

Brian and AJ looked at one another. They both knew they had to do something and fast. They'd both have to be ready for that one moment when the opportunity presented itself, to make a break for it.

Snake Eyes Bob was standing closer to Brian, so he would become Brian's responsibility. AJ was standing closer to Deacon so he would be AJ's responsibility. The sheriff was going to be the problem because he was standing farther away and holding the rifle on them.

"You boys go and get your horses while I hold these two here," the sheriff said to Deacon and Bob.

Suddenly the situation had changed. Now it was two against one, but the one was holding the gun. Still, the odds had changed in favor of the Sackett brothers.

Deacon and Snake Eyes took off to catch their horses. They had only been gone about a minute when the sheriff spotted a rider atop a distant hill.

Not wanting to be seen in the company of the Sackett's he ordered them inside the house.

"Hurry up, get in the house," the sheriff snapped.

AJ and Brian cast a quick look at one another. This could be the chance they were looking for. They moved as one towards the door and just as they entered the house, AJ grabbed the door and pulled it shut, leaving the sheriff on the outside.

Brian dropped the bar across the door to keep it from being opened and they looked around for anything they could use as weapons.

The sheriff, not wanting to open fire on them due to the man on the ridge, ordered them, "Open the door. You can't go anywhere. Open up."

"You come in and get us," Brian said.

"If I have to I'll burn this house down. I don't need it," the sheriff said as he gave a quick look see towards the distant rider.

While Brian kept the sheriff in conversation, AJ was looking frantically for something, anything to defend themselves with. He found it under the bed. It was a double barreled shotgun.

AJ grabbed the gun and broke it open. It was empty, but there had to be some shotgun shells somewhere.

Quickly AJ began going through cupboards and when he opened the third cupboard door, hit pay dirt. A box of birdshot; it wasn't what he had hoped for, but it would be a lot better than nothing at all.

AJ quickly loaded the shotgun and moved to the only window in the front room of the small cabin like structure. Obviously the sheriff had forgotten about the shotgun or didn't know it was there. Otherwise he wouldn't have been trying to look through the front window like he was.

AJ and Brian moved to points in the room where the sheriff couldn't see them. When the sheriff's shadow, however, was cast through the window due to the position of the morning sun, AJ knew he was looking through it.

The roar of the shotgun blast was like a clap of thunder as AJ jumped in front of the window and fired both barrels of the shotgun. The force of the shotgun blast coupled with the flying glass from the window sent the sheriff flying backwards off the small porch and onto the ground. His face was gone and he was dead.

Quickly AJ reloaded the shotgun and prepared for the other two to open fire. When he and Brian took a quick look out the window they realized that Deacon and Bob had not returned yet with their horses. They wasted no time in rushing out to where their pistols lay on the ground.

Deacon and Bob heard the report of the shotgun and Bob, who had been able to catch his horse, rode back to check on the gunshot. When he saw Brian and AJ running out of the house and Sheriff Joe Dean lying dead on the ground he panicked.

Snake Eyes rode back to where Deacon was and had him swing on behind him. They were able to ride up alongside Deacon's horse and he mounted it from Bob's and the two of them kicked them into full gallop.

Brian and AJ ran to where they had left their horses, mounted up and gave chase. It was evident that Deacon had been in this area before. Deacon knew the best route to take to the border. Fear drove Deacon and Bob, and anger and resolve drove the Sackett brothers.

Deacon and Bob topped a ridge and disappeared over the crest. By the time AJ and Brian reached the top of the hill Deacon and Bob had vanished. There was dust still hanging in the air, but there were three different arroyos they could have taken.

AJ was slightly ahead of Brian and reined up before motioning for Brian to take one arroyo and he would take another. They split up and rode at breakneck speed down the arroyo they had chosen. Both arroyos the Sackett brothers were in ran into dead ends.

Brian reined his horse around and galloped back to the entrance of the arroyo just as AJ arrived at the mouth of the one he had entered. Without a word they both reined their mounts into the mouth of the remaining arroyo.

They saw the horseshoe prints quickly and knew they were on the right trail then. They had lost valuable time, however, and not knowing the area found it very hard to make it up.

After a mile or so AJ reined up and called to Brian, "Hold up. It's obvious they're headed for the border. Slow down and let our horses catch a breather," AJ said.

"Yeah, I think you're right. They're not headed for town, that's for sure. Especially since they don't have the sheriff to cover for them," Brian agreed.

AJ sat for a moment and then said, "Well, little brother...it looks like we're going to be in Mexico for awhile."

Brian looked at his brother and nodded slightly and said, "Si."

***Raymond D. Mason***

# Chapter 21

**Silver City, New Mexico**

It was nearing nightfall when the carriage carrying **Black Jack Haggerty** and **Bonita Brand** arrived in the rough, tough town of Silver City. The sheriff was a man by the name of Harvey Whitehill and he had succeeded in taming the town, somewhat. His deputy 'Dangerous Dan' Tucker was also a man to give a wide berth to if you were looking for trouble.

Haggerty dropped Bonita at the best hotel in town and he took the carriage to the livery stable and boarded the three horses; the two horses broke to harness and his stolen saddle horse. He started back down the street to the hotel when he met the sheriff and his deputy.

Tucker, the deputy, looked at Haggerty with a curious eye as they met on the boardwalk. Sheriff Whitehill was busy looking through saloon doors and merely cast a glance in Haggerty's direction.

As the three men passed each other, Haggerty eyed Tucker and didn't notice the badge when he said, "What are you looking at?"

Tucker stopped abruptly and glared at Haggerty and said, "What was that?"

"I asked you what you are looking at," Haggerty snapped.

Sheriff Whitehill now became interested in Haggerty. When Whitehill turned so Haggerty could see his badge, the bad man backed off slightly.

"Oh, I didn't see the badges," Haggerty said.

"Why should that make a difference? All I did was look in your direction," Tucker said still wearing a scowl.

"I don't like people staring at me, that's all; nothing personal," Haggerty said and started to walk on.

"Wait a minute; where do you think you're going," Tucker said. "We're not through here."

"I am. I have a beautiful woman waiting for me in the hotel down the street here and she hates to be kept waiting," Haggerty stated with just a hint of a smile.

"Go ahead," Whitehill said, giving Haggerty a head nod.

Tucker looked at the sheriff and then back at Haggerty as he said, "Don't get in any trouble; not if you know what's good for you."

Haggerty clenched his teeth in an effort to hold back his anger and hatred for 'star-packers'.

"I'll tell you what, Shorty; if I decide to start trouble I'll look you up and start it by beating you to a pulp, how's that?"

Without another word, 'Dangerous Dan' Tucker hit Haggerty in the stomach with a punch that doubled him over. Tucker whipped out his pistol and hit Haggerty over the head with it, knocking him out cold.

Whitehill looked at Haggerty and then at his deputy, "Dan I wish you wouldn't do that when someone merely speaks to you the wrong way. Now we have to let him sleep it off in the jail."

"You know I don't let anyone talk to me like that, Harvey."

"Yeah, I know. Well, you knocked him out; you transport him to jail."

Tucker reached down and pulled Haggerty to his feet and laid him over his shoulder. He headed down the street getting stares and comments from men he met along the way.

"Who's your friend, Dan," one man asked with a chuckle.

"May I have the next dance, Dan," another man Tucker met said; obviously men who were on good terms with the five foot seven inch deputy.

The next morning Haggerty woke up with a splitting headache. He let out a low moan when he tried to sit up and the sheriff walked to the door separating his office from the cells.

"Well, I see you finally woke up. After you've had breakfast I'll let you out," Sheriff Whitehill said.

"What happened," Haggerty asked with his eyes closed as he felt the tender knot on his head?

"You met my deputy...the hard way."

"If it's all the same to you, Sheriff, I'd just as soon skip breakfast and go back to the hotel room I haven't even been in yet," Haggerty said.

"Sure, if that's what you want. If I was you, though, I'd give my deputy a lot of room. He doesn't like you," the sheriff said.

"I'm not all that crazy about him either."

The sheriff walked over and unlocked the jail cell and stood aside. Haggerty picked up his hat and started out towards the main office.

In the cell next to Haggerty's was a young man sound asleep. Haggerty noticed as he walked out.

"What's that kid doing in here," Haggerty asked?

"He's in for stealing something. He's not a bad kid; his ma is the biggest problem with him. She's a prostitute and he has no guidance what so ever."

"Does this bad guy have a name," Haggerty asked?

"Yeah he does...*William Bonney*. I just call him *'Kid'*."

The sheriff followed him and walked to his desk to take Haggerty's gun and holster out of the bottom drawer.

"What's your name," the sheriff asked before handing Haggerty his gun and holster?

"Haggard, Jack," Haggerty said.

"How long are you planning on staying in town, Haggard?"

"Not long. My...lady and I are on our way to Tucson. We're going by horse and carriage and will be leaving tomorrow morning. You wouldn't happen to know how far it is, would you, Sheriff?"

"Yeah, it's around a hundred and forty miles. Take water with you. Enjoy your stay here, but be careful," Whitehill said.

Haggerty nodded and held his hand out for his gun and holster. The sheriff handed them to him and watched as Haggerty checked the cylinder to see if his gun was loaded.

"It ain't loaded. Do so after you leave this office. If you fire that pistol in town you'll be spending another night in jail," Whitehill said with a grin.

"Adios," Haggerty said and walked out.

Haggerty had just reached the hotel entrance when he met Bonita coming out. She gave him a stern glare as she snapped, "Well, I hope you had fun. I sure didn't."

"Hey, I spent the night in jail, if you must know. I've got a bump on my head the size of a goose egg and I don't need any lip from you," Haggerty snapped back.

Bonita looked shocked and then asked, "Let me see."

She tenderly put her finger on the knot Haggerty was sporting and then looked sad as she said, "I'm sorry. I thought maybe you'd met another woman. I'm the jealous type when it comes to my man."

Haggerty merely nodded and said, "Let's put on the feedbag. I'm hungry."

After Haggerty and Bonita had eaten a good breakfast, Jack told her to go shopping because he had a couple of things to take care of before they left town. He gave her enough money for a good shopping spree and he headed off to check out the freight office.

Haggerty had every intention of picking up some easy money before heading on to Tucson. He'd spotted the freight office when they rode into town the evening before. Once he had a chance to case it, he felt sure he could handle the job by himself.

Walking around to the back of the freight office, Haggerty saw the way he could get in easy enough. The building had a loft in it. Perhaps it had been a barn before it became the freight office, but there was a hay loft door at the top near the eave of the roof.

Haggerty noticed the beam that was used to hoist hay up to the loft sticking out a good five feet above the loft door. He could easily throw a rope over the beam and climb up to the loft door. It shouldn't be too hard to get the door open and he would be inside the freight office. As far as the safe was concerned, he figured he could crack any safe built.

Haggerty waited until he figured the freight office would be closed and the people gone home for the night. He didn't want to say anything to Bonita about his plans; the less she knew the better. He'd make an excuse for going out and she'd be none the wiser.

The freight office closed at six o'clock at night. There was a night watchman, but he was seventy eight years old and hard of hearing. Haggerty didn't know that, however. He also didn't know the old man had been an Indian fighter in his younger days.

Haggerty went to the livery stable and picked up his lariat from his saddle and took it back to the rear of the freight office. He'd need it to get up to the loft door and didn't want Bonita to see him with it and start asking questions about it. He found a place between a rain barrel and the freight building wall to hide it.

After Haggerty and Bonita had eaten a late supper, he told her he wanted to play a couple of hands of poker and would be gone for no more than an hour. Although Bonita wasn't too happy about it, she agreed to it when Haggerty told her he'd buy her something very pretty with his winnings.

He walked her back to the hotel and checked his watch against the clock in the hotel lobby. He wanted to have some sort of alibi about where he was at the time of the robbery should that question come up. It was exactly eight thirty.

"I'll be back here by nine thirty, honey," Haggerty said.

"Bring a bottle of wine from the saloon, so we can have our own little party, Jack," Bonita cooed.

"That sounds like a good idea to me," he said with a grin.

He gave her a kiss and took off down the street in the direction of several saloons as well as the freight office. When he looked back, Bonita was watching him. He gave her a wave and when she waved back, she went in the hotel.

Seeing that she was no longer watching him, Haggerty quickly turned down a breezeway between two buildings so he would be in back of the freight office. He didn't want anyone seeing him anywhere near the place.

Haggerty quickly recovered the rope he'd stowed away and under the cover of darkness lassoed the hoist beam. He looked all around to make sure no one was in the area and then began climbing up the rope.

When he reached the loft door he swung out away from it on the rope and as he swung back towards it, gave the door a mighty kick. He had halfway expected the door to fly open, but it didn't.

Again, he swung out and once he'd swung back in the door's direction gave it another hard kick. This time the door gave quite a bit. One more good kick he thought should do the trick.

He shoved himself back away from the wall and just as he started back in the direction of the door, the back door to the freight office opened. It was the night watchman coming out to see what the banging against the building was all about.

When the old man saw Haggerty swinging out on the rope, he yelled up at the man. Before Haggerty knew what had happened, the old man raised the double barreled shotgun he was carrying and fired both barrels at him.

The blast hit Haggerty in the back, knocking him to one side and causing him to lose his grip on the rope. The blast had done a lot of damage to Haggerty and the fall added to it. He hit the ground hard, bleeding profusely from 'double ought' buckshot.

Haggerty hit the ground with a dull thud. The outlaw trail that 'Black' Jack Haggerty had been riding came to a swift end. He was dead. His lifeless eyes stared up at the night sky. It was now time to pay for the sins he had committed against his fellow man.

The old man walked over to Haggerty's body and looked down at him. As he stood there peering down, the sheriff rounded the corner of the building in a run. When he saw the old man standing there he slowed and then looked at the dead man at the old mans' feet.

"What happened, Sam," Sheriff Whitehill asked?

"This man tried to rob us, Sheriff, and I was forced to shoot him," Sam said.

"You sure did a number on him," the sheriff said as he looked closer at Haggerty's body. "Hey, I know this man. He and his lady were on their way to Tucson. I guess I'll have to locate her and give her the bad news," the sheriff said.

"Don't know about that," Sam said. "I just know he was trying to rob us."

The sheriff noticed the rope hanging from the hoist beam, but didn't say anything. He wasn't even sure whose rope it was and right then didn't care. He grabbed a wheelbarrow that was next to the building and loaded Haggerty's body into it.

"I'll deliver this guy over to the undertaker. I'll need a statement from you about the shooting later, Sam."

"What was that about underwear, Sheriff," Sam asked, cupping one hand behind his ear?

"Nothing, Sam. I'll see you later."

"If you want me to make out a statement, Sheriff, see me later," Sam said loudly.

# Epilog

**Brent** and **Julia Sackett** were on their way to California with Grant Holt and his infant daughter little Gracie. Now they had the Thurston children as well whom they had taken in. Denver Dobbs may, or may not, be a problem for Brent. Only time would tell.

**Brian** and **AJ Sackett** were heading into Mexico in pursuit of Rawhide Deacon and Snake Eyes Bob for shooting John Sackett, their father. Because AJ had shot and killed the sheriff of San Felipe del Rio in self defense the two brothers would undoubtedly have to face charges when they came back to the United States side of the border.

**Linc Sackett** still had a man filled with hate for him who was bent on evening the score for Sackett killing his friend. Linc now had another problem to deal with; Miss Shauna. Buck Benton would not take kindly to her having eyes for his top cowhand.

**'Black' Jack Haggerty** had been killed and his story brought to a close. He'd died the way he'd lived, by the gun. His killer, however, wasn't another bad man, or a marshal, or even a gun fighter, but an aging, hard of hearing Indian fighter by the name of Sam.

## The End

**Next in the Sackett Series:
"Between Heaven and Hell" (Book # 6)**

## Books by This Author

### Mysteries

8 Seconds to Glory
A Motive for Murder
A Tale of Tri-Cities
A Walk on the Wilder Side
Beyond Missing
Blossoms in the Dust
Brotherhood of the Cobra
Counterfeit Elvis: (1)
Corrigan
If Looks Could Kill
Illegal Crossing
In the Chill of the Night
Most Deadly Intentions
Murder on the Oregon Express
Odor in the Court
On a Lonely Mountain Road
Return of 'Booger' Doyle
Send in the Clones
Shadows of Doubt
Sleazy Come, Sleazy Go
Suddenly, Murder
The Mystery of Myrtle Creek
The Secret of Spirit Mountain
The Tootsie Pop Kid
The Woman in the Field
Too Late To Live

### Westerns

Aces and Eights
Across the Rio Grande
Beyond the Great Divide
Beyond the Picket Wire
Brimstone; End of the Trail
Day of the Rawhiders
Four Corners Woman
Incident at Medicine Bow
King of the Barbary Coast
Laramie
Last of the Long Riders
Man from Silver City
Night of the Blood Red Moon
Night Riders
Purple Dawn
Rage at Del Rio
Range War
Rebel Pride
Return to Cutter's Creek
Ride the Hard Land
Ride the Hellfire Trail
Showdown at Lone Pine
Streets of Durango: *Lynching*
Streets of Durango: *Shootings*
Tales of Old Arizona
The Long Ride Back
Three Days to Sundown
Yellow Sky, Black Hawk

# Book Series:

## Frank Corrigan Series:
Corrigan
Shadows of Doubt
The Return of Booger Doyle
*Next in series to be published:*
*An Invitation to Murder*

## Nick Castle Series:
Brotherhood of the Cobra
Beyond Missing
Suddenly, Murder
*Next in series to be published:*
*The Cardiff Affair*

## Dan Wilder Series:
A Walk on the Wilder Side
Send in the Clones
Murder on the Oregon Express
A Tale of Tri-Cities
Odor in the Court
*Next in series to be published:*
*To Mock a Killing Bird*

## Rick Russell:
The Mystery of Myrtle Creek
If Looks Could Kill
*Next in series to be published:*
*Riddle: Diamonds and Gold*

## Quirt Adams Series:
The Long Ride Back
Return to Cutter's Creek
Ride the Hellfire Trail
Brimstone: End of the Trail
Night Riders
*Next in series to be published:*
*Quirt Adams, Outlaw*

## The Sackett Series:
Across the Rio Grande
Three Days to Sundown
Ride the Hard Land
Range War
*Next in series to be published:*
*Five Faces West*

## Streets of Durango Series:
Streets of Durango: Lynching
Streets of Durango: Shootings
*Next in series to be published:*
*Streets of Durango: Bounty*

## Luke Sanders Series:
Day of the Rawhiders
*Next in series to be published:*
*Moon Stalker*

*Five Faces West*

Printed in Great Britain
by Amazon